Gertrude of Stony Island Avenue

Gertrude of Stony Island Avenue

A Novel

James Purdy

William Morrow and Company, Inc.   New York

Library of Congress Cataloging-in-Publication Data

Purdy, James.
Gertrude of Stony Island Avenue : a novel / James Purdy.—1st
U.S. ed.
p.   cm.
ISBN 0-688-15901-X (acid-free paper)
I. Title.
PS3531.U426G47   1998
813'.54—dc21   98-10746
CIP

Printed in the United States of America

First U.S. Edition

1   2   3   4   5   6   7   8   9   10

BOOK DESIGN BY BERNARD KLEIN

www.williammorrow.com

For
Miss Abercrombie,
John Uecker
and
Matthew Stadler

Gertrude of Stony Island Avenue

Daddy is very peevish and irritable. He thinks I may be writing something about Gertrude. I, who seldom had the patience to write a postcard to anyone, and of course more trouble writing a letter. All I do is jot down little notes—recollections of Gertrude. Daddy complained once I sat up late scribbling. "Come to bed, Carrie, like a good wife and helpmeet."

Daddy is failing. Oh, is he ever. What will I do when he is gone? And the chilling thought came to me like someone whispering behind my armchair: *You will write down everything you can remember, Carrie, about Gertrude, your daughter, Gertrude of Stony Island Avenue, Chicago.*

We never got on, Gertrude and I. Yet I believe we loved one another. I often sit all day thinking of my own failings. Daddy knows this and it makes him even more irritable and bad-tempered. "You should take up your music again," he scolds.

He and I both sang once in the church choir, that is where we met, in fact. And we also sang for a while in the chorus of the Chicago Opera, oh so many years ago I shiver to recall.

Daddy found some of my notes about Gertrude. To my surprise it did not make him too angry. But he would not say what he thought. Daddy's lips now form one very thin bloodless line. The doctor mentioned his pale lips, and when the doctor mentions anything it means there's something wrong. He never mentions anything good after his examination.

"Daddy will be leaving me," I keep saying, and my voice chokes. (I do talk to myself more and more.)

And when Daddy goes, how strange, there will only be Gertrude to occupy my thoughts with.

She was not a beautiful girl. Her chin was too pointed. I even once thought of plastic surgery, for the rest of her face was quite lovely with beautiful large green eyes, and lovely Titian-colored hair. Her skin would have been more pleasing had she not been such an inveterate sun-bather. It was her body that attracted the men. And it was men that occupied most of her time when she was not painting her peculiar oil portraits, portraits which now hang in many of the world's museums. I never liked them. I still do not. I am only responsive to the Old Masters, but as she once said to me, "That's because you don't even know how to look at them."

I sometimes think she had so many fellows because it was her way of spiting me.

Daddy and I never discuss her penchant. It was the word Daddy once used for Gertrude's many love affairs.

And it was from one of her many boyfriends that I heard used the phrase *one-night stands.*

"All you are good for is one-night stands, Gertrude," I heard this young man say to her as I was about to rap on her studio door. They heard somebody outside and I scurried away. I think Gertrude knew it was me. I was not eavesdropping (she later accused me of this), I was about to knock, but couldn't bear to let her know I had heard what I had heard. She thought I did not know what she did when she was not before her easel. Men men men. She could not get enough of men. Daddy knew it, but I think Daddy has this great gift I do not possess, he can shut his eyes to almost everything he does not want to think about.

It was Daddy who persuaded me at the beginning of our courtship to attend the Plymouth Brothers Church, but I was a poor believer.

I don't think Daddy knows he is failing. And I don't think as a result that I know he is. He looks despite the mask of age over his face like a young boy at times. When I note that youthfulness on his face he stirs and gazes at me with a troubled frightened expression.

"What is it, Carrie," he will say. "What is on your mind?"

"Nothing at all, Daddy," I always reply. "Don't you worry now."

He smiles then a grim smile. We both know things are changing.

"I am surprised," he began today at the breakfast table,

"surprised you spend so much time going over Gertrude's effects."

"Oh, it only passes the time," I tried to solace him.

"Eight hours is a long time for that," he quipped.

"There was a lot to Gertude's life we know nothing about, Daddy," I finally remarked just for something to say.

"Don't delve, Carrie, whatever you do. Please don't. Let the dead rest in peace."

I suddenly broke into tears.

"Why, Carrie, what have I said to make you sob. I ask you!"

"Nothing that you said, Daddy," I went on.

I felt I was doing wrong, but I could not help myself. If Daddy was not failing perhaps I could not be delving into Gertrude's life, and especially her young men.

Once when he was in one of his brighter moods, he said, "You forget, Carrie, that the young men our Gertrude knew would not be young today."

"Oh, I know, Daddy," I replied.

"But you don't act like you know," Daddy went on, and he took out his pipe against doctor's orders, and lit it. I said nothing about his disobeying medical instruction. Indeed I welcomed the sweet tobacco fragrance.

"They would be old, most of them," Daddy returned now to the mention of Gertrude's beaux.

"Oh, Daddy, you act as if I was going to run after them."

"You're seeking information, Carrie. But why?"

I tried to think up an excuse, but could not.

"Go ahead, tell me, why don't you."

"Oh, they know things about her, Daddy, we never dreamed of."

"Carrie, Carrie, you act like my little girl."

"I wish I was," I replied. "I am so wretched, so very wretched."

I should not have said that. It brought Daddy up with a start. I could see him trying to garner up his energy to say something to encourage me.

Finally he said, "You have to do what you can do, for look at me, would you, just look."

"Don't speak that way, Daddy, please."

"Just look at what has happened to me, Carrie, I am not me any more."

"You are to me," I almost shouted. "Yes, you are."

"Time certainly plays a joke on one," he spoke more quietly now and blinked his eyes.

"Let me take your pipe, Daddy, for it's gone out."

"All right," he said in a put-on cross tone. "Do what you want to. You will anyhow. Visit them if you want to. Why mind me."

"Visit whom, Daddy, for heaven's sake."

"The young men who are now old."

"Oh, go on. Where would I find them? They may be dead, too. Who knows?"

"Some of them would be around," Daddy reflected. "And I know you need a pastime. When I look in the mirror I always say, Carrie needs someone more than me to take her time up with. So, visit them. See if I care. You seem to forget that I am ten years older than you, Carrie. Time has a way of doing with us what it pleases."

"I never think of you as older."

"Well, maybe then you should think again."

We sat then very quietly together and almost content.

"Oh, Daddy," I said as I turned on the evening lights, "so you think I should go look for the young men who were her beaux!"

"You should get out of the house. One excuse is as good as another. But I have to grin when I think you are going to be a detective."

"A detective," I pretended to be indignant. "How can you say such a thing even in jest?"

"Searching out the lost lovers!" He laughed his old deep laugh, and I felt almost happy then. It was like long ago when we were young married people.

○

The next day I began going through what Daddy called Gertrude's effects. But instead of finding anything of value my hands came across some old photos of Daddy when he was courting me. I was stuck dumb by the photographs. Daddy looked far more handsome than I ever remembered him. His eyes, especially, were to me the most beautiful of any man's I had ever seen. And though the photo was black and white, it caused me to remember that Daddy's eyes had a real gold tinge to them. But even back then I noticed his face was more heavily lined than a young man's of twenty or so usually is. And today Daddy's deep lines are so pronounced one feels they could lay a finger in any one of them.

I can hardly explain the deep depression which fell upon me as I looked at those photographs. I hurried with them to a seldom-used chiffonier and hid them away in a heavy wooden shoe box.

Daddy noticed something was wrong.

"What have you found now snooping around," he wondered. Against doctor's orders he was drinking a huge cup of black coffee. I said nothing for awhile until I heard his sharp "Well? What have you found."

"I found Gertrude's wedding ring," I lied. (Actually I had come across it the day before and had quickly put it away in the same chiffonier where Daddy's youthful photos now rested.)

"And that depresses," he asked. He knew I was lying and I don't know why I was telling an untruth. Somehow I could not bring myself to tell him about his photos for I knew he would want to see them, and when he saw himself in his wonderful youthfulness what might it not bring on. A relapse, I was afraid.

"You have secrets," he spoke almost inaudibly, mournfully.

"No, Daddy," I responded. "Not real secrets."

"I forgive you, Carrie." He finished his cup of coffee.

That morning we rented a limousine and drove through Jackson Park. At the end of the ride Daddy said he wanted to get out and have a look at Lake Michigan. The driver helped him out. I stayed inside the car, and suddenly burst into a kind of tempest of crying.

When Daddy came back he stared at me for a full minute, and then taking out a handkerchief from his breast pocket he handed it to me for drying my face. One of Daddy's ways is he always has a large collection of pure Irish linen handkerchiefs. He is never without one.

I had to bite my lips, however, as I dried my face not to begin crying even harder and drenching the handkerchief with my tears.

Then there was the affair of the intercepted letter. That was the beginning of everything changing.

"Do you want me to mail your letter?" I inquired when I saw it was lying on the little hall table, and had not been posted for a couple of days.

"Let Maud post it when she comes." (Maud was our cleaning woman.)

"But this is Friday night, Daddy. Maud won't be here until late Monday."

"There's no rush for it," Daddy muttered. "It's not important."

"But I'm going out now for some groceries, Daddy. I can post it."

"Suit yourself," he spoke in an angry uncivil tone.

"Why, Daddy!" I showed my hurt.

"Post it, damn it, then. Post it! I told you 'tweren't important. Or tear the damned thing open if you like. Now leave me alone, Carrie, I'm trying to snooze here by the grate fire."

I did not reply. But when I took the letter in my hand, I saw it had not been properly sealed. The contents of the letter came out in my open hands. I could not help reading it. I mean I could not stop my eyes from taking in the short contents.

The letter was to Daddy's attorney, Hal Winterrowd:

Dear Hal,

Under no circumstances confide in Carrie about our daughter's past involvements. She would worry herself ragged, and then her worry would compound itself on me. Carrie's very close herself to a nervous breakdown. I am not either in the best of health. Mum's the word. As my most trusted confidant, remember: silence.

Yours,
Vic Kinsella

I stood motionless, the open letter in my hand.

"Are you still in the hall, Carrie?"

"Yes, Vic," I replied, using the name he had used in his letter to Mr. Winterrowd.

"Well, close the door when you go out. I feel a draught. And what's this tack of calling me Vic all of a sudden?"

"All right, Daddy. I'm going now."

I put the letter deep in my outside coat pocket.

"How will I seal the blamed thing," I spoke out loud to myself.

"Carrie," he shouted.

"Yes, Daddy."

"Are you speaking to me or mumbling to yourself?"

"Myself, Daddy. I'm going now."

Outside I wondered what to do about sealing the letter. I felt guilty as sin. But more than guilty I felt hurt and mad. And what did he mean I was near a breakdown! I saw all at once he respected and confided more in a common lawyer than his wife of forty years. Some tears stood in both the corners of my eyes. But even more than this hurt was a sickening apprehension Mr. Winterrowd and he knew more about Gertrude than I had ever been allowed to share in. I recalled now Daddy's anger when he found me going through Gertrude's effects.

"Gertrude had a secret. Many secrets." I heard myself talking to myself, and the postal clerk smiled as he overheard me.

"Of course we can seal the letter, Mrs. Kinsella," he was saying. "Give it to me." He put some thick yellow paste where it had come open.

"Oh, thank you so much," I told the clerk. "My husband forgot to properly . . ."

I did not finish my sentence. I knew the postal clerk had heard me talking to myself, and I blushed for the first time in I don't know when.

The clerk took the sealed letter, and it was gone.

A nervous breakdown! I almost shouted the words as I reached the street. He has his nerve to say such a thing.

A smart not so much of sorrow but slow rage came to my eyes.

I felt Daddy had betrayed me. I felt he did not love me. And I was to my astonishment jealous that he felt something also for Gertrude he had never felt for me. That in fact he loved Gertrude more than he loved me.

The man in the post office knew something was wrong with that letter. Oh I felt I should begin then keeping a diary as Gertrude had, but then Daddy or somebody else would read it, and think I was crazy.

And now I must tell that Gertrude's own diary was not like any diary you have perused or peeked into. It was largely, queer as it may seem, a collection of names, addresses, and odd half sentences like:

*Pratt has very pronounced sideburns which
give off the faint perfume of lily of the valley.*

Of course I must keep in mind Gertrude was in her day a famous painter and used live models.

So I went on trying to explain these haphazard discon-
nected comments she had written like this:

His face had the texture of an overripe
sunflower head.

or:

The broken nails on his sinewy toes
cried out for a sculptor, not a painter.

"Daddy must never see into Gertrude's diary," I was
speaking aloud again now to myself. But let me correct
the term diary. It was not a diary at all. It was well, why
not say it, a book of codes. Unspoken, never to be uttered,
half-finished notes to herself like someone talking in sleep
or in the shadow of death.

Many years before I found my mother had kept all her
notes to the milkman, such as:

Two quarts of your farm-fresh buttermilk.
Don't forget either the pint of smearcase you
promised last Thursday, and please, would you
seal the bottle more securely.

Oddly enough Gertrude's jottings in her big maroon
leather book reminded me of my poor mother's notes to
the milkman, and what surprised me in my mother's case
was she kept these notes to the milkman in a little drawer

of her kitchen cabinet. Why did she keep notes when they were no longer of any use to the milkman or her. I had always wondered. And now, why had my Gertrude left these half-finished, usually unintelligible, sentences for whose ever eyes they would fall on.

But she must have meant the book to be destroyed!

Just before her last hours she had left word something was to be destroyed.

For a long time after reading *"His iron nipples gave me a vision that has never left me"* I was afraid to go on reading her diary.

"Mama, you are so sheltered, dear heart," Gertrude had once told me, and then she kissed my hand.

"What do you mean by that," I wondered. "You see things," she said, "like a young girl of ages ago who has never ventured out of the front door."

I laughed uproariously over this comment, and Gertrude joined in.

"Did you post the letter?" I now heard Daddy's voice.

"Of course, Daddy! What do you think I am? Would I throw a letter of yours in the dust bin?"

"Good Lord, what a peculiar remark to make to your husband."

"You and that Hal Winterrowd," I said. "I declare!" But I spoke too low probably for Daddy to hear.

"Do you miss Gertrude," I asked Daddy as I was finishing manicuring his nails. Daddy cannot use his right hand very well, and perhaps even less his left one. There were two things Daddy always insisted on with regard to his toilet. He shaved daily (he had rather a heavy beard), and he kept his hands in an immaculate condition for a businessman. They did not have a manicured look for Daddy prided himself on his masculine appearance, but they looked handsome. Now he cannot of course tend very well to these things. Our servant, Maud, shaves him sometimes, but more often a young Greek barber comes and does this.

"Why do you ask me such a thing," Daddy pounced on me and drew his left hand out of my grasp.

I had almost forgotten what I had asked him, there was such a long lapse of time after I had put the question to him.

"Do I miss her," he repeated my inquiry. "What nonsense women talk!"

"That is not nonsense, Daddy, and you know it."

"Well, do you miss her," he almost roared at me, and began drying his hands. After a while he lowered his voice a bit to say, "Gertrude has been dead two years now."

"It seems a hundred, Daddy. To me, of course."

"To tell the truth, Gertrude was not easy in my company," he spoke in that strange faraway voice he used now. "She had many outside interests in any case, whatever she may have felt for us."

"What do you think she felt for us, Daddy?" I began putting away the manicuring set.

"There you go again, that blamed talk all you women have!"

Grinning slightly, he said, "She was a very active person," and then surprisingly enough he blushed. I stared at him so hard he blushed even more furiously.

"Gertrude did not confide in me, Daddy. I tried time and again to win her confidence, but to no avail."

"Do you know what it was, Carrie?" He spoke in an almost loving, ever so soothing manner. "She was devoted entirely to her painting. Her painting was her life, not us."

"Gertrude painted from life." I spoke now like an unwilling witness in a court trial.

I saw immediately that what I had said annoyed Daddy. He looked at me with fierce wonderment and almost terror.

"Could you explain what you really mean, Carrie," he mumbled, and he did not look now in my direction.

"Why, she told me time and again she painted from life, Daddy. Behind the closed doors of her studio." I was lying and he knew I lied, why Gertrude never said anything to me about her painting or the young men who posed for her. I got this particular information from a gentleman who was viewing her paintings in a museum show.

"You mean, don't you, she used live models," Daddy prompted. "As any artist does."

"As any artist does!" I flared up. "Gertrude was not any artist. I'm surprised to hear you say such a thing."

He painstakingly took off his glasses now and looked at me, and in that look for a brief moment I saw the golden eyes of his young manhood, and I could not help making a kind of brief sobbing sound.

"We can't understand artists, Carrie," he mused, still gazing at me. "Certainly I don't."

"Where do you suppose she got her calling, Daddy?" I began carrying out the water in the basin to a little lavatory in the next room. I listened to the water gurgling down the drain, my back to Daddy.

"She would have to go and paint," he sighed. "At least we weren't fools enough to stop her. What good would it have done? Gertrude always went her own way in the end. She had a strong will."

"How right you are there, Daddy." I could not resist the impulse now to go over and kiss him right above his eyes.

He smiled then and tried to take my hand in his, but he was not able to. I pressed his bad hand gently, and his lips moved in a half-smile.

Then a change occurred.

When I heard Daddy say the words "I don't think I'll go with you this morning for our drive, Carrie," I felt as if a hand had clutched my throat and would not let go. He was not looking at me as he said this or he might have noticed the effect his words were having on me. But when I said nothing in return, he looked up and after mumbling a bit, he managed to get out, "You'll enjoy getting a little change of scenery in any case!"

"But I've never taken the ride without you, Daddy, you know that."

I tried to keep my voice calm and my hands quiet but I could do neither.

"The motion of the car," he began, "it's not good for me now."

"But why didn't you tell me, Daddy? We don't have to take the ride if it makes you feel bad, for heaven's sake. And besides, why should I go driving alone?"

"Because I want you to, Carrie. It's you who needs the ride."

"I?"

"Cooped up here day and night with a sick man, for crying out loud. Go and enjoy it. Go to Washington Park, too, why don't you? Do you know Washington Park has a thousand acres, including woodlands and more than a few lagoons, and statues of war heroes? You could get out, Carrie, and take a short stroll."

"Daddy, Daddy, you know perfectly well it is not safe to walk there."

He did not hear me.

The bell rang. It was the driver.

He was a different driver from the one who usually called for us. He silently helped me on with my coat.

I felt then that I was going on a long journey. I had never had such a feeling of bereavement. I could not believe Daddy's excuse that the car made him queasy. But what was it, then?

"Take good care of Mrs. Kinsella," I heard Daddy's voice instructing the driver.

17

When I was seated in the roomy back of the limousine, I remembered I had not said good-bye to him.

"What did you say your name was," I asked the new driver.

"Marius," came his answer and he tipped his cap. "Where would you like to go, ma'am?"

"Didn't Mr. Kinsella tell you where," I inquired.

"He did, ma'am, yes."

I said nothing, my thoughts were back with Daddy.

"Washington Park then, ma'am?"

I nodded in agreement, and Marius started the motor.

Coming back from my drive, I found Daddy seated in the same chair he had occupied when I left.

When I went over to greet him, I realized he had completely forgotten I had ever been away.

"I have been thinking, Carrie," he began.

I encouraged him with a smile to go on.

"At my time of life," Daddy began hesitantly, "there seems to be left only diversion, what they call killing time. The diversions which fall to my lot are not anything I precisely am interested in, but at the time I think what else is there? When we are young we are so alive we never think of diversion. Everything we do is bubbling over within us. We glide with life. We are not waiting for life, or planning for some distant future. We are life."

He gave me a questioning troubled look.

"Now don't start contradicting, Carrie, or I will send you out of the room."

❀

A day or so passed then. I don't know if I was surprised
or not, but Daddy all at once seemed strong again, even
well. He issued commands, told me to wear my hair
shorter, insisted again that I take a drive every morning.

"And stay away from this sad place, do you hear? For
at least two hours get a change of scene!"

"You want to be alone, Daddy," I spoke more to myself
than to him. But Daddy heard me.

"No, I don't want to be alone especially, but I can't
bear to see you grieving over what can't be helped. You
know what I mean. That driver, did you say his name
is Marius, he will come every morning at ten, Carrie,
and you should remain away till you get tired. Make it
as I said two hours. You have got to get out of the house,
do you hear? Breathe fresh air, see fresh faces, whether
strangers or friends."

I hardly heard what he was saying. He rattled on.

❀

Then there was the coming of Gwendolyn!

"She had so many names, had been married at least
four times. Or who knows," Daddy remarked, "the number might be six." She was Daddy's younger sister. Much
younger to hear her story. She had married wealth with a

third husband, great wealth. I think he was an Englishman. And they lived in Paris, until his demise.

Gwendolyn had never cared for me. I was not her kind of woman. She as good as said so. She looked spuriously young. Must have had her face lifted several times. Used thick powder and paint and false eyelashes. Very expensive hair dye which would have fooled even a hairdresser, but though her hair seemed the genuine shade, still her face despite all she had paid to make her look young, sometimes was after all that of an old woman. At least to me.

"Gwen is coming here for a visit," Daddy said one morning when I was waiting for the driver.

His news made me so unhappy I could say nothing.

"Did you hear what I said, Carrie?"

"Daddy, lower your voice. Of course I heard you. What am I supposed to say?"

"You'll have some company besides me."

When I was silent: "You may not get along with Gwen," he spoke cautiously, pausing, "but she will nudge you maybe into not being so teary and sad."

"Oh, Daddy, I declare! Teary, my foot."

"Well, you look like a paid mourner most of the time."

"Gwen has your cutting tongue, Daddy. I see where it comes from now."

"She is a caution," he admitted. "But she's all I have . . . from my own family," he quickly added.

"Yes, we need our family, certainly," I managed to say.

The bell rang then, fortunately. It was Marius of course,

and I was so flustered with the news about Gwen I left the house again without saying good-bye to Daddy.

"Gwen!" I spoke her name aloud before I even got in the car that morning.

"Did you say something, ma'am," Marius inquired. But then he knew by now I talked to myself.

"My sister-in-law is coming to visit us," I explained. "Gwen, from London."

"That will be a change." The driver sounded almost boisterous. "Will she be coming for the morning drive with you, ma'am?"

"I hope not," I spoke in a peevish way. "She's lived most of her life abroad. Most of it in Paris. I'm afraid Chicago will be a comedown to the likes of her."

We drove on then in silence.

◦

I began to change still more—I suppose for the worse. I thought of myself all at once as a desperate woman. Then smiling a strange wry smile such as I had never worn before I added the word *desperado*. And a *thief*. By a thief I mean I went boldly one day into his den where he kept all his private papers and while our cleaning woman looked up in amazement I opened the big drawer marked PRIVATE, DO NOT DISTURB, and took out what I knew must be Gertrude's private RECORD BOOK. The cleaning woman kept staring at me in shocked disapproval, but the look on my face, my new wry smile I had never had before, prevented her from speaking. Just as I was about to leave the den I turned back and said to her, "We ladies have our own reasons, don't we, Maud?" To my relief she smiled and nodded.

Back in my own room I looked hungrily through the Record Book. I kissed its torn smudged pages. But what were those stains I wondered, which appeared on many of the pages? Wine, blood?

"My only dear," I kept repeating as I searched through Gertrude's crabbed almost indecipherable handwriting.

"My lost lost child," I said. I was beginning to say everything aloud that came to mind. From the years of keeping everything to myself or saying only what Daddy might approve of I now began speaking all those words that I should have said to Gertrude when she lived.

My eyes were too dimmed with sorrow to go on reading.

And I knew now, trembling, that I feared and hated Gwen. She looked down on me, pitied me, felt supremely superior to me. She and Daddy had always put their heads together. In times past they discussed me by the hour, listed my shortcomings, my careless attention to my clothes and my hair, my plainness, my lack of being able to carry on a conversation. Then after their raking me over the coals, Gwen would always end her put-down of me with the words "Of course Carrie is as good as gold, we must remember that. We could hardly do without her, could we, Vic?" And I could just imagine Daddy beaming and nodding then on his sister's insincere hollowed condescending praise of me.

I went on pouring over the Record Book, but my mind was elsewhere. It was as if I were suddenly Gertrude, for Gertrude had not written down complete thoughts, only little phrases. Scholars might think them hieroglyphics. As I tried to piece out what she meant, I suddenly said aloud: "I hate Daddy. And I loathe and despise his sister. I wish she was dead, coming here to afflict and torment me by looking down on me, pitying my provinciality, my having never done anything."

"She is hardly a conversationalist now, is she?" I could hear her voice downgrading me. And she and Daddy had both laughed shrilly at this remark of hers.

I felt a little like the day when Gertrude, angered by my silence and my failing to pet and hug her, had taken up one of her cut-out dolls I had given her and set fire to it with a kitchen match.

I was too horrified to stop her which made her dislike me the more.

"I do not like paper dolls," she had screamed at me.

"Do you hear me?" Gertrude had raised her tiny three-year-old lungs. "I do not want dolls made out of paper!"

"What do you want, child," I had whispered.

"A real-life mama," she had said.

Then blinded by her own tears she had come over to me and laid her head on my long taffeta dress, and we had cried together, but we were not together, we were crying like two people not only in separate rooms, but in separate houses. She knew then and I knew also we would never be able to love one another, though this was the one thing both of us wanted.

Gertrude's Record Book, despite its incomprehensibility, became a kind of Bible for me. Every page was short, almost unintelligible, yet I read and reread what she had written. I studied her Egyptian hieroglyphics. The more I studied, the less I cared about Daddy or his vile sister who was coming to harass me.

I had found my vocation, my calling in the vespers of my own life, my life's purpose in dead vanished Gertrude.

○

Whether it was Gwendolyn's coming or because I was out of the house on my rides so frequently, whatever the cause Daddy was looking stronger, more like his old self. His voice had regained in part its timbre and volume. He walked up and down in his den a great deal.

Shortly after my "theft," Daddy summoned me to the den with a note passed on to me by the cleaning woman who had caught me taking Gertrude's Record Book.

The drawer out of which I had taken the Record Book was still ajar when I entered the den. I have never had any histrionic ability, certainly was not gifted in playing the hypocrite. But today I was the most finished actress who had ever trod the boards. I merely glanced at the open drawer and then as calm as Ethel Barrymore, said, "What is it now, Daddy, dear?"

I felt at that moment as if I was about to roll a cigarette like one of the heroines in a recent movie I had taken in on the sly.

I saw that my calm and collected, my cold demeanor, had floored Daddy. He could think of nothing for a time to say.

"Have you nothing to tell me, Carrie," he spoke in a crestfallen, desolate manner.

The thought of Gwendolyn's coming and her long years of unkindness gave me a clue. I spoke in the coldest manner I believe I had ever displayed to my husband.

My "no" to his question was so perfect in its frigidity and control, Daddy's mouth dropped almost to his handsome cravat.

"I am expecting the chauffeur, Daddy." I rose. My eyes barely glanced at the open drawer.

"So please, then, dear, let me know how I can serve you," I managed to add as I turned toward the door.

"Something is missing, Carrie, from my papers," he spoke now in a half-apologetic manner, as if he and he alone was to blame.

I took up this drift, and said, "You have never been too orderly, Daddy." I turned now and grasped the doorknob, holding it lightly in my left hand. "I'm sure it will turn up where you have misplaced it."

But the look of utter astonishment that swept over Daddy's face almost made me lose my own poise.

Even more brazenly then I blew him a kiss.

As soon as I had regained my own part of the house, a sudden fit of laughter overtook me. But it was, I knew, not real merriment, and sounded to my ears more like a strangling cough . . .

Yet, I had triumphed. I understood then a little of what thieves and other criminals say they experience when they have been successful in a crime.

It was my hatred of Gwendolyn which allowed me to be so abandoned and unpenitent, yes, but it was also something else. It was the expression on Daddy's face, the look of pure astonishment which made me savor my victory.

He had deprived me of my daughter, he had taken Gertrude away from me at an early age. He was the thief, not I. By reclaiming her Record Book, I had only taken back in a small way what should have always belonged to me. I could not ever have the flesh-and-blood Gertrude, for he had stolen that from me. I was within my own rights to take possession of the often meaningless scribbling and secret codes of the Record Book for my own.

"No man can ever be as close to a child as a mother," I spoke aloud. "Yet he ousted me from that place in Gertrude's heart!"

A surge of some unfamiliar emotion swept over, and like a doer of misdeeds I was again proud of my theft, proud of my defiance.

For when my sister-in-law came now she would not find the meek and cowed, awkward and shy, irresolute and quaking Carrie of old, but rather a lioness deprived of her cub.

☙

Sometime in the far reaches of night I heard the door to my bedroom open softly. My sense of hearing had grown seemingly more acute during Daddy's illness, and then also I never slept the whole night through. I could hear his breathing as he closed the door behind him and stood at the bedside. I pretended I was fast asleep. But Daddy like me is always aware of when his spouse is pretending. Daddy knew me, he once said, like a watchmaker knows the inner workings of his timepiece.

Daddy knew I was a thief, Daddy knew I was playing opossum now.

"Carrie, Carrie," came the inconsolate cry. "How could you step so out of character? How could you walk off with Gertrude's Record Book, willed to me by her hand?"

My breathing became more labored, but I held myself motionless otherwise.

He slumped down on the bed, and slowly took my right hand in his.

"Now when she is gone, you show all this interest in her. Now she is just dust you shower her with attention and concern. Oh, Carrie!"

I moved slightly under his pressure. We had not slept

together since Gertrude's death and I was dreadfully afraid he would want to be intimate with me. I think had he tried I would have run out of the house and down the street.

"So you are not asleep, then, are you?"

I could not have replied even if I had wanted to. It was as if an iron glove throttled me.

"My poor girl," he began again after moving away from me and seating himself in an armchair. "You need not see Gwendolyn at all if she is so distasteful to you. I want you to be comfortable. I know you no longer love me, of course. I wonder if you ever did. Probably not. I know too of your long suppressed anger against me, Carrie. I may live on and on after all, to make you miserable. The doctor marvels I am still tough as nails. But I am no longer me. No longer at all. We can cancel Gwendolyn's coming if she spites you so much. Little she would care. Do you know of her life, Carrie?"

Somehow at this dead time of night Daddy was more open in speech and thought than he had ever been in our daylight hours. Yet I kept as still, as motionless as if I heard not a word he was saying. And I feared if I let on I was listening to him I would break out into a tempest of recrimination and diatribe, even cursing.

But finally I heard myself say, "You are not I."

"I know that, dear heart," came his cry of relief and perhaps a faint kind of joy. "Oh thank you for speaking. See here, you did take the Record Book. Why not admit it?"

I nodded.

"Thank you, thank you." He sounded, despite the firmness of his voice, very old. Perhaps it was because I could not see him that the character of advanced age was even more noticeable in his speech with its groaning hesitation between the words.

"You may keep it, Carrie. I will not need it. But why could you not have asked for it? I would have willingly given it to you."

"No!" I raised up now and almost shouted. "You would never have given it to me. It is too late for lies, Daddy. Too late."

I pressed my nails hard into my palms. "Too terribly late!"

"I wish you would give me another chance," he said after a lengthy silence. He rose then.

"Don't go, Daddy. After you have broken my sleep and come in here, more like the thief you accuse me of being. Now you are here and I am wide awake, have your say out. Torment me some more, you who stole Gertrude from me before she could even walk or talk. Yes, you are the thief!"

My anger could no longer be reined in.

When I felt he was holding me to his chest, I pushed him away.

Still standing close to me he said, "So you have never been happy with me, Carrie. Tell me the truth."

"I don't know the truth, and never did," I managed to say. "I am like Pontius Pilate."

"Do you want to leave me then and go live by yourself, Carrie?"

"I do not. I will live here until the end. And I may die before you. In any case I am dead already."

"Carrie, Carrie, mind what you are saying."

"That is you talking all right. You have never allowed me to say anything I really felt or thought. That is the man of it anyhow. We must speak according to his tenets and hidebound rules."

"Shall we talk in the morning then, Carrie?"

"No. I will be going for a long drive tomorrow."

"May I kiss you good night, Carrie?"

I pushed my face toward him and he hesitated a long while before I felt the touch of his cold lips.

"Good night then, Carrie, and excuse me for disturbing you."

I was unable to reply.

○

Gwendolyn, Gwendolyn! She was to be my penance, the Nemesis of all my failings and shortcomings. Sent by some pitiless justice from only God knows where. She appeared, it seemed to me, with drawn sword and in armor. She barely looked at me as she pronounced sentence. She issued one command after another. I was to be her prisoner and her ward, her aged child and her final mission and task in life.

She went to work with a grim kind of zest. I was to be her final accomplishment, her limitless task, and that task

had behind it all the energy and knowledge of her many
years.

No one knew how old Gwendolyn was, not even Daddy
was clear on this point. She might have been—oh why con-
jecture. She looked, however unbelievably enough, somewhat
young, perhaps ageless is the right word. Yes, she had no
age. Like the goddesses Hera and Artemis, about whom I
was to learn later, she might have been in the Greek section
of a great museum, privileged for awhile to be alive for certain hours of the day in our own world and time. To partake
however briefly of our own pedestrian life.

She kissed me that day as she entered my private room
and almost dislocated my arm as she took my hand in hers.

"We will set to work, dear sister. Fear nothing." She
spoke in a kind of baritone, perhaps even a high bass. "All
can be resolved," she went on. "Shall be resolved. We must
save Vic if only to let him see the change in you. For you
will change now I am here. I have not the slightest doubt
of that."

I felt then like a prisoner being visited by the severe but
kind judge who had done the sentencing in the first place.

"We will begin at the beginning, my dear," she said.
The words *my dear* came from her mouth like the most
calamitous swear words.

I tried not to gasp as I heard her speech, and she embraced me again.

"All will be well," Gwendolyn encouraged me, and then
went out from my cell as miraculously and noiselessly as
Athena herself.

I picked up the soft satin pillow nearest me and held it against my face. It gave off a faint odor of some flower whose name I could not recall. All at once I felt a vivid shivering sensation come over my whole being. I pressed the pillow tightly against my breast until the sensation subsided.

Yet another part of me rejoiced that Gwendolyn had arrived, had come to perform my punishment. I saw that I had awaited her coming all my life.

I had ruined my daughter's life. I had propelled my husband into a fatal illness. I had tarnished my own life, and had refused happiness whenever it made its appearance.

All this was revealed to me by Gwendolyn's arrival.

Judge, jury, trial lawyer, she fulfilled all roles, and having signed my death warrant she appeared high above as some kind of angel who would perhaps if she so deemed reinstate me in her own realm, bestowing on me the chance for a bitter but perfect redemption.

I rose and managed to reach my bed. I was too weak to put on my nightclothes, almost too weak to turn back the counterpane of the bed and stretch into the white cotton sheets. A thin streak of saliva stained the pillow slips, and I sank into a kind of slumber.

I was awakened some hours later by Gwendolyn, who now sat beside me, a steaming cup of hot broth in her hands.

"You must renew your strength, dearest sister," she began, but the word *sister* in its monumental falseness brought on another crisis in me. I screamed and cried, but

Gwendolyn paid not the least attention to my outburst, forcing down the medicinal broth through my clenched teeth and lips.

Yes, it was true. The broth and whatever it contained made me as quiet and docile as a child who has just nursed at its mother's breast. I sank into the first beneficial calm I had experienced in years.

○

Even before Gwendolyn came I was changing. I vaguely perceived it, but a thousand other things were struggling for recognition, things I had kept down and hidden inside of myself.

Since Daddy's illness, Reverend McKnoll had been visiting him, but his visits with Daddy—short ones—were always followed by a conference with me. Reverend McKnoll had suggested that he and I read the Scriptures together. He felt this would give me strength in the face of my worry over my husband's sickness.

I remember that our lesson on this particular day was the "Parting of the Red Sea." But it was also a day or so after Gwendolyn's arrival.

Her presence, her extravagant personality seemed to dominate Reverend McKnoll's own behavior, even his appearance.

As he began to explain what the parting of the Red Sea meant, I took a close look at him, covertly of course, but with a kind of concentration on my part which finally brought a faint blush to his youthful cheeks. For Reverend McKnoll was at least to me a very young man. He could not have been more than thirty-five.

I heard little or nothing of his explanation of the parting of the Red Sea, for my attention was on the small veins above his right eye, and the larger pulsing veins in his neck. For the first time perhaps in my life I became aware of what Gwendolyn must have known all her own life and which she would have brazenly referred to as male pulchritude. Reverend McKnoll was extremely handsome. And like me, vulnerable. I tried not to stare at him or even look at him at all during the lesson. In vain. My eyes rested finally only on him. Finally he blushed furiously.

"You must help me, Reverend," I heard my own voice.

His mouth opened as if it was his mouth which would receive the explanation of my strange behavior.

"You have only to call on me," he managed to say, while holding in his outstretched hands before me the enormous Holy Bible.

"You have no idea," my voice ran on, "how much these visits of yours do for me. I am so grateful." I put my own hands under the Bible as if to lessen the weight of it in his own grasp.

I thought he now became rather pale. He was, for a few minutes, almost at a loss for words.

Then he began speaking quickly, volubly, about the hidden meaning of the parting of the Red Sea.

I nodded almost on his every word, but my eyes were

now on his rather heavy beard which no daily shaving could quite efface.

From his nostrils I also noted wirelike very black hairs emerging and moving slightly under his troubled breathing.

Reverend McKnoll's breath now came—so it seemed to me—in thick heavy gasps.

Finally almost leaping up, he rose and said he must leave to visit another of his parishioners.

I sat motionless a long time after he had departed. I do not even recall having given him my heartfelt thanks or accompanying him to the door.

It was as though under the influence of Gwendolyn I had imagined his being with me at all or explaining the mystery of the Red Sea.

But what the Red Sea's parting meant as far as I was concerned was that there had begun to be a change in me as cataclysmic and earthshaking as the upheaval of the sea itself.

I was on the other side of my old life. I was hurrying off to some uncharted world, leaving Daddy and finally even Gwendolyn behind.

They were now on the other side of the sea, and I was alone with the woman I had always failed to recognize, the woman who was me.

Gwendolyn looked at least thirty years younger than her calendar age. I did not want to know how she had achieved this. Actually I did not even want to know anything about her. But since I had seen her some ten years earlier, she had undergone a complete metamorphosis. I would not have recognized her on the street or in a social gathering. She was entirely different, totally new.

"Gwendolyn," I would often begin speaking her name, and she would nod encouragement.

"I have forgotten what I wanted to ask you," I would reply. Then Gwendolyn would smile and take my trembling hand in hers.

I was still daydreaming—yes that is the word—about Reverend McKnoll when I came out of my absentmindedness long enough to see that Gwendolyn had come into my room without my realizing it. How long she had been sitting there holding an unlighted French cigarette in her mouth I did not know. Furthermore she was talking a blue streak.

"Why don't you light your smoke," I interrupted her. She ignored my reference to her gold-tipped cigarette.

Daddy had forbidden her to smoke while staying with us, but in the usually empty little bathroom down the hall (Gwendolyn called it her W.C.) I often smelled the fumes of her latest indulgence.

What on earth was she prattling about now, I wondered, with the unlighted cigarette all the while between her lips.

"She ruined my life." My attention revived on hearing

these words coming from her. "But from those ruins I became me."

"Who are you talking about now?" I raised my voice and stood up for a moment, but the sight of her angry expression caused me to sit down immediately like a schoolgirl corrected by the principal.

"I am trying to tell you about my life," she began all over again. "A life which at your present stage you can not understand. For if you ever want to understand your lost Gertrude"—she almost lunged forward at me as she said these last words—"then you have got to listen to me whole-heartedly, with rapt attention. Are you going to listen or aren't you? Shall I get up and leave you to your bawling and sobbing and feeling sorry for yourself? Or will you hear what a real life such as mine is about?"

I welcomed her rudeness.

"Let me hear you out, Gwen."

She gave a kind of a grunt of a laugh at this statement.

"The *she* I have reference to is of course Annette Smith. When I say, however, she ruined my life, I mean she destroyed the poor simp I was in that prairie town I came from and instead made me a flesh-and-blood woman. What hicks here call a woman of the world, or a cosmopolitan, or probably an adventuress. For without Annette Smith, I would have remained in the airless motionless town and probably cut my throat in the bargain."

The life of Annette Smith was, of course, right out of the Sunday paper supplements of long ago, along with "true life" accounts of human vampires and ax murderers.

Annette, like Gwendolyn, like Daddy, had been born in a tiny Midwest landlocked village, or in Gwendolyn's phrase, a prairie crossroads. Unlike most of her girl companions, Annette's sole interest was not in sewing or church socials but unmarried young men. And even a prairie village had a surplus of farmers, wheelwrights, even blacksmiths—ignorant but endowed with the fresh sap and tireless vitality of the soil itself. At the age of thirteen she had learned to make her own dresses, had studied makeup from a lady barber, plucked her eyebrows, had begun smoking imported cigarettes, and having made Gwendolyn's acquaintance at a harvest-home dance, had insisted Gwendolyn visit her heiress aunt who lived in a thirty-room mansion from which one could see the distant Ohio-River. The aunt must have known that Annette brought young men to the upper story of her mansion. Like Annette herself, her aunt smoked one imported cigarette after another, and was frequently visited by a young Danish doctor who administered her an opiate for her headaches. The aunt, dying of boredom, welcomed the influx of youth and gaiety from her niece and her young men took a special interest in the as yet virginal Gwendolyn.

"I did not need much coaxing," Gwendolyn's voice purred on, "for with Annette as my teacher, I found total surrender in lying under the bodies of the young men whom Annette lured to her aunt's mansion."

In all this rambling interminable repetitive often boring but to me spellbinding narrative, my own mind came to a full stop like that of a broken heirloom clock.

Annette, Gwendolyn's idol, teacher, and gadfly, was to my sister-in-law the luckiest woman who had perhaps ever lived, certainly the luckiest to come from an obscure prairie village, and at the age of fifteen, left for London, where she went through at least four successive husbands, all immensely wealthy, and of whom one was said to be of noble birth. Her greatest achievement came when she married—so Gwendolyn's story went—the son of the Tiger of France who had helped frame the Treaty of Versailles.

At this point in her story I felt her shake me.

"Are you listening or shall I leave you now for my smoke in the W.C.?"

"You may smoke here, see if I care." I thought my voice sounded very much now like hers, cold, vibrant, pitiless.

Gwendolyn burst into what was to my ears a horselaugh.

"You take the cake," she muttered.

"I followed in her footsteps," she began again now on Annette, but she pointed to a handsome settee, and suggested I sit there with her for the narrative to come.

"I followed in her footsteps."

As she spoke these words I felt Gwendolyn's arms about me, as on and on went the story of what the world calls a woman's ruin, but to Annette and Gwendolyn was rebirth, glory, matchless splendor.

Gwendolyn, like her idol Annette, could barely remember when she had been a virgin. And whenever she uttered Annette's name, she let into her voice a kind of awed tremolo such as one might employ in addressing if not the Virgin Mary, Venus herself.

I saw then that perhaps the only person Gwendolyn had ever loved or looked up to was the international adventuress Nettie Smith.

The story of Annette and Gwendolyn gave me, I believe, the greatest torment and anguish I had ever known with the possible exception of Gertrude's death. No, Gwendolyn's narrative unhinged me more thoroughly. I do not know why to this day.

She and Annette had lived to the full—they had never refused any of the pleasures or ecstasies which this world can offer. Perhaps that was why I felt such torment, yes, such envy, jealousy, fierce stifled rage. They have lived, not I. And like them, my Gertrude had also lived, the Gertrude who had hated the paper dolls which I had given her. Gertrude had gone on to life, leaving me in the smoking ruins of Daddy's real estate business and my conjugal fidelity.

But my tears had evaporated. My tear glands had become paralyzed.

Instead I would give out an occasional quiet laugh as Gwendolyn sped on and on with her story. This pleased her. She would smile and despite her facial surgery thousands of wrinkles would suddenly take over her million-dollar mask. She would then hold me to her. And her caresses, her kisses even, galvanized my attention to her saga of depravity and international swindling.

I found now I could be at ease with her because, as I realized, she inhabited a world beyond my wildest suspicions. I could no longer care as a result what I said or even did in her presence, any more than when once I had briefly conversed with Galli-Curci, the great Italian diva, as she emerged from a private carriage, my sudden surprise at seeing so great a star allowed me unbidden to kneel before her and kiss her gold-spangled gown. Galli-Curci in response kissed me full on the lips.

"Tell me more about Annette." I heard my own whispered words as I relived my encounter with the divine Galli-Curci.

"Tell me more about Annette," I heard my own improbable plea.

And her narrative would begin again. And I had never dreamed I would know anyone who not only had witnessed these depravities, even crimes, in the highest social echelons of Europe but who had lived through them to come to enchant and disorient me with them. I, who in her words still dwelt in a prairie village.

"It is your hick quality, your utter ignorance of anything but your own deadly dull origins, which endears you to me!"

Gwendolyn's very insults relaxed me, made me tolerate her.

One day as her story-telling was continuing I found I had fallen asleep in her arms.

◗

"I am very concerned that Gwendolyn upsets you so much."

Daddy was at his most pontifical. He made me feel that

the headmaster of a private school had called me into his office to have it all out with me.

And I realized perhaps somewhat to my disappointment that Daddy did not look so ill anymore. He looked almost robust. And I felt this recovery was the work of his sister. Bad as she was, she had revived, restored him!

"Why does she upset you so much," he pursued his examination.

"I never said she upset me, Daddy. Please!"

"But Gwendolyn says she upsets you."

"Ah," I flung at him. "That is another matter."

"What do you mean by that?"

"She is not truthful. She babbles. Can anyone take in all the ocean of words which continually comes out of her mouth. I am reeling, I tell you, from listening to her. There is no end to all she tells. She has lived the life of twenty women and those twenty women are whispering in my ears twenty-four hours of the day. I am drowning in her outpourings."

"We can ask her to stay in a hotel, Carrie. Or we can ask her to go back to Paris."

"I don't want her to leave."

"But if you are reeling!"

"I deserve then to reel. Deserve to be made miserable by her. Yes," I went on as if I was in my private room talking to myself, "I deserve to be made wretched. She is necessary to me. But I have also the right to complain about her. About my own dull backwoods life as she calls it. You, too, Daddy. She considers you living in the back-

woods also, a provincial, a hick. She says there is nothing
wrong with your health but that you and I are both dying
of incurable boredom."

"I am surprised then you want her to stay on with us."

"I am surprised at myself, Daddy."

"Oh you women. God help us!"

"Let me tell you something, Carrie." Daddy now became confidential, and whispered. "I hardly know my own
sister. She ran off from home when she was a mere child.
Sixteen is a mere child at any rate in my book."

"But," I interrupted, "she claims there was a young
woman who gave her the nerve or maybe the excuse to
leave home."

"So, she's been telling you then about Annette." He
gave a kind of snort and then giggled embarrassedly.

I saw the reference to Nettie Smith had stirred something deep in Daddy. Probably he had not even heard the
name of his sister's friend for many decades.

"I don't think," he began to muse now, "there was ever
a girl so lost to decent behavior as that young girl." And
then Daddy smiled broadly. As I had never seen him
smile before.

"Let me tell you," he warmed up to the story. "She
went to England with hardly enough clothes to cover her.
As she told Gwendolyn at the time, she didn't need clothes
to make her fortune. She became the toast of London during the First World War. Married one of the country's
wealthiest men. Divorced him, married another, even
wealthier. Oh I can't recall all her vicissitudes. But her

final triumph was when she landed the son of one of France's greatest statesmen."

"The son of the Tiger of France," I prompted.

Daddy stared at me with something like pride or admiration.

"So she has been taking you into full confidence."

After a long silence in which he appeared to be living back in the days of his own youth, he said, "So now you know it was Nettie Smith who was the architect of my own sister's checkered career."

Though I thought I didn't want to hear all the details of the lives of these two women whom Daddy called harpies, I didn't want him to stop talking. Just the sound of his voice calmed me, as the sound of radio announcers dialed low often put me to sleep. In the beginning twilight of my life I required the sound of the human voice. Listening therefore just to Daddy speaking was sufficient for my nerves. "I no longer cared or could keep count of how many times Nettie Smith and Gwendolyn had marched to the altar and signed the marriage registers," Daddy's voice pursued.

"Why our Gwen has had so many husbands," I caught a snatch of Daddy's monologue, "she can't at a moment's notice recall all their surnames."

I laughed heartily for me at this last sentence.

"Then shall we allow her to stay?" He searched my face for an answer.

"You make the decision, Daddy, for heaven's sake."

"Oh well, tell her yes," I said when I saw the look of hurt and disappointment coming over his face.

"Tell Gwen for me, we welcome her under the same roof."

"We'll put her on trial, then," he suggested.

"Oh, trial nothing, Daddy. Good grief, she has brought fresh air into the house even if that air has, as you say, its origin in unspeakable behavior."

Daddy closed his eyes and made a sound almost like that of purring.

◯

I seldom now slept the whole night through, but instead of finding sleeplessness disagreeable, I welcomed these long hours of insomnia when the whole city outside was quiet and Daddy and Gwen were also no longer talking and spatting or loudly renewing their memories.

It was then I got a kind of irresistible urge to visit the den again. I felt there was something more to discover there, something tempting, forbidden, perhaps even electrifying.

I searched for my old soft slippers, but they no longer fit. I walked barefoot to the den.

To my surprise the door was partly ajar.

I opened it a little wider, afraid Daddy might be inside snoozing.

There was nobody there, but a night lamp was burning.

No more Record Books of my daughter, no more any-thing to tempt the eye until almost ready to leave I spotted a great pile of yellowing papers.

It was almost too heavy to pick up, and I almost slipped on the buffalo robe under my feet and then slumped down with the mystery sheaf into Daddy's armchair.

The papers had the title *AN INDEX OF THE FOR-GOTTEN ITEMS OF AMERICA.*

Like Gertrude's diary and Record Book these countless pages (later I was to find reams more) were a collection of phrases, dates, names of disappeared celebrities, old silent movies, opera divas, prizefighters (the Argentine Firpo for one), and scattered bars of once popular music. Each page had the words "Compiled by Victor Kinsella."

"Why," I said aloud, "have you never told me about this, Daddy?"

In my rattled state I guess I expected my absent spouse to reply.

Then, wouldn't you know, I went and dropped the whole stack of pages.

It took me nearly an hour to put them together then, but in my disturbed state I realized it was impossible to put the pages back in proper order again.

Staring at these new hieroglyphs I felt I was further distanced from Daddy, that he had in a sense joined Ger-trude in a realm I could never reach or be part of.

I longed to weep or cry out, but, as Gwen had remarked, my weeping and crying days were past.

I went on staring at the stack of pages.

Forgotten phrases, I muttered, disappeared celebrities. I thought again of my own meeting with Madame Galli-Curci which seemed as remote and nebulous as something I had merely imagined.

I heard a noise in the hall. I trembled with a fear like that which an inexperienced burglar might feel. But the noise in the hall stopped.

My bare feet were now icy cold, and I had an urge to cough. Restraining the urge to do so, I bit my lips till they hurt.

An hour or so later I found I had fallen asleep in Daddy's chair. Looking outside I saw that it was getting light.

I rushed out of the den and with fortune on my side, got to my own room without being discovered.

I realized then that Daddy's thousand-page pile of notes meant something deep, but I was equally sure he was never going to tell me what the thousand pages meant. Only Daddy knew the secret. And I, as usual, was shut out from finding the meaning of what Daddy had laboriously written over the years.

I felt the temptation then stronger than ever to visit the den again and take down Daddy's manuscript. Why should his own wife not be told of its existence? Why oh why was I shut out from everything?

I waited that night until everything was quiet, then I walked again in my bare feet to the den.

The thousand pages appeared to be waiting for me.

This time I was careful not to drop them. They seemed heavier than ever as I took them down from the shelf.

Looking closer I was suspicious they had been looked through recently, for they were not now in the neat and orderly arrangement I had left them in.

I wondered if Gwen had visited the den and looked through the pages.

Then my gaze fell on a large drawer slightly ajar. I had never noticed it unlocked before. Impulsively I yanked the drawer open. Inside—and it was a deep drawer—I saw huge stacks of what turned out to be more pages of *The Forgotten Items*. Did I say there were a thousand pages of the items? With this new discovery I put their number at ten thousand! I slammed the huge drawer shut containing my new find and again fell heavily back into Daddy's armchair.

After a time I resumed my reading of the pages I had found on the shelf.

I leafed through them slowly almost sleepily. I came across:

RECOLLECTIONS FROM THE FUNNIES

The Katzenjammer Kids. Why couldn't I have had boys like them instead of . . .

Don't Forget Dinty Moore's

And I would have liked to have known Moon Mullins and The Widow Zander & Kayo and Lord Plushbottom and Emmy.

My eye took in the names:

Billy Sunday, Baseball Star Turned Evangelist

Diamond Jim

THE PICTURE SHOW

Pearl White, Mary Pickford, Alla Nazimova, Jeanne Eagles

Jetta Goudal, film beauty. What if I had known her. Find out more for these files

There was a long list of other forgotten silent film stars, then came a list of baseball players, such as Ty Cobb, Walter Johnson, and Christy Mathewson. Heavyweight boxers were listed, like John L. Sullivan and Jack Johnson, and the Argentine Firpo.

I felt frustration, too, for Daddy's handwriting was so poor in many places I could not have deciphered it. A magnifying glass nearby only made the handwriting look more illegible.

I was, however, able to make out the name "Credit Mobilier."

There were thousands of names, forgotten stars, forgotten heroes, forgotten ways America spoke back then, yes I suppose forgotten dreams.

I sensed a terrible headache coming on. Looking up, I saw Gwendolyn had come into the room.

Unbidden she took a seat near me, but didn't utter a sound.

Prosaic, deadly boring as my life was according to Gwen, the discovery of Daddy's *Index of Forgotten Items*, not to mention Gertrude's diary and Record Book, revealed that at least to me behind all this tame, insipid life we were leading on Stony Island Avenue, there was in existence something after all mysterious, strange, and yes frightening.

Taking in my worry and my consternation, Gwen gazed at me now so searchingly I averted my eyes away from hers.

"There is only one person I know can explain it all," she spoke almost in a whisper. "Evelyn Mae Awbridge."

"Oh, Evelyn Mae, you don't say so."

"The Shakespearean authority," Gwen prompted. "But don't you know her."

"Of course I do. I have visited her house in the company of Gertrude."

"She's not only an authority on Shakespeare," Gwen reminded me. "During the war she did government research on codes."

"I had no idea of that. You're sure, Gwen?"

Gwen nodded and gave me one of her pitying smiles.

"And you think Daddy's *Index of Forgotten Items* is a code?"

"I think nothing, Carrie. Of course, we have no right to have looked into it, have we. And less right I suppose to show it to Evelyn Mae. But I do know one thing. She would give her eyeteeth to have a glance at it."

Whether it was Gwen's sudden appearance in Daddy's

den discovering me snooping through his papers or the thought of sharing Daddy's secret with someone outside our house—whatever the reason my hands suddenly trembled violently. Several pages slipped from my grasp to fall at Gwen's feet. Without waiting a moment Gwen reached down to take them.

Her attention was riveted and as she read through the pages a broad smile swept over her face.

"Carrie, Carrie, this is too wonderful to share with anyone but you."

She began reading aloud therefore the pages which had so riveted her attention.

Here I am then [Vic wrote] *at the age of thirteen, I guess. I have always been goggle-eyed by heroes, for who doesn't know I was a baseball fan from the time I could throw a ball. But all to myself, I secretly had another hero unbeknownst to my school chums. My hero of heroes was John Philip Sousa, the March King. When I learned the great leader of the band was to be in town at the local opera house, I got permission from my seventh grade teacher to attend. The audience was not made up of kids so much as older teachers and townspeople. But it was me and not them who got carried away by Sousa's band music. I applauded so loud after each number that one of the ushers gave me a disapproving scowl but I persisted over the rest of the audience who were satisfied with gentle little and almost soundless handclaps while I yelled and whistled my approval.*

Bowled over by my hero the March King, at the end of the concert I followed John Philip Sousa who was an old man even then to the train station, even offering to carry one of his valises. The old band master was taken with me (at least I flattered myself he was), and he autographed several of my programs. But what thrilled me to the marrow of my bones was that travelling behind and around the bandmaster on the way to the train were women I had never set eyes on before except maybe in adult picture shows.

Painted Easter eggs, these ladies were. Painted to within an inch of their lives, and what perfume came from their gorgeous duds. It made the hair of my nostrils vibrate as if someone held a palm leaf fan to my face. "You are a very lucky gentleman," I told John Philip Sousa and the old bandmaster chuckled. "Not only are you, sir," I went on, "a great composer and band leader, you are, I see, if you will pardon a young boy for saying so, a lover of the fair sex." John Philip Sousa then stopped in his tracks and embraced me right there on the public sidewalk in view of a big throng of onlookers.

The next morning, Gwen joined me at breakfast.

"Look here, Carrie," she began. "Let me say something at this point, will you?"

I nodded.

"I can't let you follow my brother to his grave."

Gwendolyn's voice had roused me from moiling over the narration of Daddy's meeting with the March King. I little dreamed that Daddy's encounter with John Philip Sousa would have shaken me emotionally so deeply. For here was an aspect of Daddy I had never had an inkling of in all our forty years together.

"Meanwhile," Gwen was going on, "you're still young. But what's more urgent, is you have never lived. That's right, don't look at me like that. I see now I didn't come here to make my brother's last days comfortable. I came here to save you from him and from yourself. You think I don't like you. The fact is, Carrie, I have always cared for you deeply, but you would never allow me to show my affection for you. Now I have broken with my past life, there is still something for me to accomplish, if you will let me. Oh, don't I know what you are thinking. You want to go down with him!"

Gwendolyn spoke all this very much like an old actress I once admired who always delivered an intermission speech appealing for the audience to give their undivided attention to the final act of the drama to come.

As Gwendolyn spoke to me, she took on a different character and appearance. I would hardly have known her had I suddenly entered the room and heard her oratory. I also caught a glimpse of what she must have looked like in her London and Paris days when she had turned all heads.

She hurried on with her proposals for me.

"I know you never loved Vic. Don't say anything now or interrupt me. And don't pout. Only someone who cares for you deeply will talk to you as I am now. Pouting is one of your worst faults. It is worse in my book than real misbehavior. You pout because you cannot act, cannot be you. And if you don't summon all your strength now you

may even precede Vic in death. I am appealing to you to
live. Be my pupil. You will thank me for the rest of your
life. Don't turn away from me."

She held me in her arms and pressed her lips against
my face.

"You must have loved someone once, tell me. You who
were I am told as a girl a strikingly beautiful thing. Who
was he, the one you loved?"

I had not thought or pronounced the name of Mead
Thomas for perhaps thirty years. If Gwendolyn had not
done another thing for me she brought back as from another world his name and presence.

I could not have shuddered more had my girlhood
sweetheart himself entered the room at that moment.

She studied me as a hundred forgotten thoughts and
feelings crowded my mind.

"Why didn't you marry him, then, if you loved him so?"

I forget if I told her about Mead having taught me to
swim or whether the recollection of those times I kept
to myself.

It was Mead who taught me to swim in the old Blanch-
ard River. I had been fearfully afraid of water, but in his
arms I felt I had always been a swimmer, as if I had been
born to the water of the river.

As I let Gwendolyn stroke my hair, my hair and scalp all at
once felt wet with river water, and I recalled vividly the scent
of pomade which had arisen from his yellow hair.

"And you put your fingers through his hair," Gwendolyn prompted me.

She knew everything. I even called her Circe, and she laughed in appreciation.

I felt indeed as if she was rocking me on her lap, caressing me into telling her more and more of my first and only deep love.

"And there was no one else, Carrie?"

I wanted to hurry over the rest of the story I had forgotten for so many decades of time.

"May I?" I hardly heard Gwendolyn ask my permission to light one of her French cigarettes.

It was the smell of the tobacco, for Mead was an inveterate smoker, which may have revived the recollection of what I still felt was the darkest day of my life.

And the darkest day of my life was, I now realized with something of horror, was not when Gertrude died but when Mead Thomas left town. Out of habit I went on waiting for him every evening at the Riverside Park. I refused to believe he had gone away . . . I think I waited for three hours the first night, hoping he would appear. The next evening I waited till past midnight.

My mother would stare at me during these days and nights, but she said nothing. When I looked in the mirror I hardly recognized my own features.

After the first shock and the realization he was gone, I began to make inquiries. First I went to his house where he lived with his grandmother. She was a cross and angry old woman. She would only say Mead had gone to the West Coast. He would not be back. When I asked for his address she closed the door on me.

I went to the local newspaper, the *Courier,* for I knew he had worked there off and on since he was a young boy. They confirmed his grandmother's story. They knew of no address.

I waited daily for the mailman to bring me word of him. None of course ever came.

Looking down at Gwendolyn I saw she had fallen fast asleep beside me. There was a queer sort of amused smile on her lips.

I knew then despite all my resolutions to the contrary that I was going to be close to her if only because she had brought up from the deepest part of myself the presence of Mead Thomas. She had brought back my own youth from where I had buried it I thought forever.

"Mead Thomas was the only one I ever loved," I spoke to the sleeping Gwendolyn. She gave a faint sigh.

Yes, she was changing me. I had to admit that much. And I was no longer as miserable, or as she would say using a French word, not so *déracinée* once she was under our roof.

❍

The change in me was not lost on Daddy.

Gwendolyn, he had thought, had come to take care of him. Now all she had time for was me.

I overheard their voices raised in "spats," as we called them, and which in their loudness carried even to my room.

Sentences like "What ideas are you putting into her head?"

Then everything quieted down as when a phonograph record is shut off.

I had dozed in my chair when I heard Daddy's voice.

"May I have a word with you, Carrie?"

I rose to go with him, but he said, "We can talk right here, Carrie."

He refused my suggestion he sit down. He began what Gertrude always called his infernal pacing. Finally, however, he did sit down.

"Gwendolyn is a woman of the world," he began.

I made a scoffing sound which was reminiscent, I realized, of one of Gwendolyn's mannerisms.

"All right, all right," he grumbled. "Whatever Gwen is or is not, she is not like you. You are in deep water with her. You haven't, dear Carrie, a clue to what such a woman is like. There is hardly a thing a human being can do which Gwendolyn has not done. She and Nettie Smith!" And, at the name of the latter, he let out a warwhoop. "As to Gwen, I hardly know what her last name is now. She has been married that often. I don't even know the nationality of all her husbands. What should I call her, a cosmopolitan, the smartest of the smart set. In the old days to which I am not ashamed to belong we called such women adventuresses."

Then bending toward me, his eyes smarting, his mouth closed tight, he said, "Carrie, I'm afraid you are under her spell!"

"You speak as if I had no mind of my own."

"Not at all. I know your strength and character. Your sterling qualities. You are worth ten of Gwen. But we are dealing here with a greater strength and will than either of us possess, don't you see?"

"What in creation has she got you to tell her?"

Somehow he had either overheard or Gwen had told him the story of Mead Thomas.

My mind was frozen as I mentioned Mead's name, as an arrested person finally gives out the information the officer desires, for Daddy had known of Mead also.

"Puppy love," I heard him mutter. "First infatuation."

He brought out his pipe, put the stem in his mouth, unlighted.

Then I heard him repeat, "Mead Thomas," which brought a shiver through my heart.

Daddy rose then and, bending down, kissed me lightly on the forehead.

He was at sea over Gwendolyn as much as I.

☙

Yes, I had sunk very low.

"Do you know what I think would do you a world of good?" Gwendolyn spoke to me one morning when I had finally roused myself from bed, and was sitting in my overstuffed chair. The chair had been due to be re-upholstered for years, the bottom had come out and was nearly falling to the floor, but I would not let it go to the repair man because I would have felt lost without it.

"I want to shampoo your hair and touch the color up a little," Gwendolyn spoke, in a kind of appeal.

I frowned.

"I want you to look your very best. For me, if not for yourself or Daddy. Do you hear? For me! Don't for your own sake if not for mine let Daddy pull you down to his level, as he has done all these years. Carrie, look at me. Listen, I can bring you back, do you hear?"

"Back?" I muttered and refused to look at her.

Gwen walked over to my chair and raised my chin so that our eyes met.

"Smile now, Carrie." She blew a kiss at me, and I laughed in spite of myself.

"Why not think of your swimming instructor?" she whispered.

I felt again that stab in my heart as she mentioned Mead Thomas.

"Come with me up to the little bathroom there where nobody can disturb us, will you?"

Upstairs I surrendered to her as I had surrendered the evening when she brought back the memory of my first beau and old Riverside Park.

I hardly remember the session in the upstairs bathroom. All I know is that when she had finished the shampoo I went to look in the tall mirror there.

"What is it, Carrie," she grinnned. "Don't tell me you don't recognize yourself!"

It was true. I hardly did.

"What have you done now, Gwen?" I tried to smile.

"The day will come, maybe," she said, beginning to comb out the strands of my hair and its new color and sheen. "On that day you will say, thank you, Gwen, from the bottom of my heart, thank you."

"Oh, Gwen," I took her free hand in mine. "I expect you're right.

"There is something I would like to ask you," I managed to say.

She was putting away the towels and the bottle of shampoo.

"Yes?" she said in her grand manner.

"About the papers in Daddy's den," I began, but paused lengthily.

"Well go on for heaven's sake."

"Those papers have puzzled me so."

She stared at me with an almost baleful look.

"Thousands of pages, Gwen. I had no idea Daddy was writing."

"Thousands? Yes," she sort of sighed. She had obviously rummaged through the open drawer.

"There were so many all told. Yes, I know what you're thinking, Gwen."

"I'm thinking nothing. I'm listening." Her voice quivered.

"As you know, he calls the pages an *Index of Forgotten Items*," I went on.

She put down the comb and hairbrush and kept her back to me.

"What is it, Gwen. What is bothering you?"

"Nothing is bothering me," she mumbled. "Go on with your story."

"Well then, the pages, Gwen, are sort of like Gertrude's Record Book and other things she has left us . . . phrases, names. I almost wondered if I would find Mead Thomas there."

She had turned now to face me.

"Vic always wanted to write something," she confided. "He was always writing strange little things when we were growing up together. My mother found them. She was as puzzled as you seem to be."

"What do you think he wants to do with them, Gwen?"

"What do you think Gertrude wanted to do with what she wrote," she raised her voice.

"Oh, but Gertrude . . ." I began, but a fierce look from Gwen silenced me.

"They had to put down their secrets somewhere, don't you suppose," she said.

She flashed one of her resplendent smiles. Those smiles always meant she would have no more to say.

○

I must go back a little. I had begun to engage in something which no one probably least of all Daddy would have believed I was capable of.

When Gwen finally discovered this activity of mine she denominated it my "Gooseberry Pie Period."

I had found in Gertrude's diary an old nearly-in-shreds map of Chicago. The most important aspect of this torn and aged street guide was it contained in pencil the list of all her favorite Chicago restaurants with their addresses. Most of them in the Loop. Paramount among all the restaurants was an obscure one on Dearborn Street which specialized in gooseberry pies and gooseberry compotes.

Gertrude had always hounded me to bake her a gooseberry pie. Where she got a yen for this special pastry I have no idea. And gooseberries themselves were seldom in the market. One summer however I managed to discover in an out-of-the way market some fresh gooseberries and I baked her a large pie of the fruit. The pie, however, was a failure or at least Gertrude passed judgment on it as such. I was heartbroken.

The pie was left nearly untouched.

When I saw the address of the gooseberry pie restaurant I put on one of my better muslin dresses and made my way to the Loop without telling either Daddy or Gwen.

I ate an entire gooseberry pie to the wonderment of the restaurant staff. After eating it I sat on for a while thinking of her, the map of Chicago held tight in my right hand. It was the beginning of my sampling every restaurant Gertrude had patronized. It was also the beginning of a new Carrie, for I spent Daddy's money lavishly on these eateries.

Even after I had made my trips to the Loop and sampled one expensive restaurant after another, I felt no regret at my splurging on Daddy's credit. We had always pinched pennies. Now I was spending dollars with full hands.

When I heard Daddy's voice raised in anger I presumed he had discovered my reckless carelessness with his money.

Yet I felt no guilt or shame. I did not care anymore what he thought of my acting as if money grew on trees. Let him howl. He was the one, after all, who had deprived me of my daughter. To pay him back for this I had found my mission—to go in search of my lost Gertrude, and I pressed the soiled torn map of Chicago to my lips.

As I was leaving my room, I brushed against Gwendolyn.

"Listen," she detained me at the door. "Do you hear him? Please," she spoke urgency as I shrugged her off. "Listen to me, Carrie. Be careful, be very careful. He is on the warpath."

"No, Gwen, I have been careful all my life." I held the map of Chicago before me. "It's too late for careful."

"I'm telling you, he's in the worst temper I've ever seen him in. Talk about a bull in a china closet!"

I walked into the front parlor from which Daddy's cries of rage were issuing.

"He's done it!" he shouted, but did not look in my direction. "I'm a ruined man. And I'm left holding the bag."

Daddy now brandished a sheaf of papers in the air.

Gwen, who now entered, even cringed a little as Daddy continued his outcries.

"He would have to go and die, wouldn't he, when all my affairs are in total disarray!" He struck his fist with the sheaf of documents.

"Vic, for God's sake, will you tell us who and what you are raving about?" Gwen had the courage to go directly up to him.

"Raving, is it?" He turned his fury against his sister. He came very near slapping her with the papers he was holding.

"Hal Winterrowd! That's who I'm raving about!"

"And?" Gwen had now regained her composure.

"Hal has had the selfishness and inconsiderateness to die, that's what. There was furthermore nothing wrong with his health. He died on purpose if you ask me!"

Both Gwen and I were unable to restrain a few short snickers.

"Laugh away, you vixens," Daddy went on shouting. "And what am I to do now, will you tell me? To whom can I turn? That young jackass Cy Mellerick has been appointed to take his place on La Salle Street. Calls himself an attorney. Hardly out of short trousers. How can he right what is wrong in my estate, I ask you?"

Daddy now fell into a nearby armchair and blew his nose.

"I am at my wits' end," he spoke into his handkerchief.

"I am surprised at you, Vic." Gwen ostentatiously lit a cigarette in defiance of her brother. "There are certainly a dozen competent lawyers who can take over where Hal Winterrowd left off. And, if I know anything, he was no genius. Certainly never noted for his industriousness or savvy."

"But a mere booby handling my affairs, Gwen," Daddy spoke now more peaceably, even perhaps pathetically.

He put both his hands over his eyes, then withdrew them suddenly as his anger mounted again.

"Not only my financial affairs are at stake, but there is another thing. For some years now," he spoke sotto voce as if only Gwen should hear what he was about to say. "There is the very private, confidential and, at this time of my life, pressing matter of the papers Hal and I have been working on for at least twenty years. Never have mentioned it to anyone before. My research if I can call it that of the forgotten items as I believe old Hal named them. Yes, he always referred to them, I suppose jocosely, as my *Index of Forgotten Items.*"

Gwen and I gave one another the kind of look passengers on the *Titanic* must have exchanged as they saw themselves sinking under the polar sea.

"But I see as usual," he scoffed, "that you ladies don't know what I'm talking about. It was Hal's and my most ambitious project. Now it's short-circuited, wrecked, yes, cut to ribbons, call it anything you care to. May as well throw it in the furnace and be done with it. Twenty years' backbreaking toil for nothing. Died to spite me, damn his soul."

Without warning Daddy rushed out of the room.

Gwen came over and embraced me. But we were snickering, too, as well as alarmed.

Only a few minutes later Daddy reappeared in a frayed

evening-wear suit which must have been older than his *Index of Forgotten Items.*

He threw down in front of me a series of bills which I had incurred at the restaurants in the Loop.

"And will you gaze at this lavish expenditure from my lawfully wedded wife?" Daddy addressed Gwen instead of me. "Is it any wonder I am on the road to bankruptcy?

"Listen, if you will, to the names of the posh restaurants and cafés my wife has been frequenting. The Auditorium Dining Hall, spiffy Henrici's on Randolph Street, the Blackhawk where they dance till dawn, the Drake private dining room, the Persian Room, the Golden Ox, the Blackstone! The Palmer House! And of course Mrs. Krantz's Ice Cream Parlor on Randolph Street favored by Mrs. Potter Palmer herself."

He glared at me for a moment then turned back to his sister.

"She has been dining out as if she is married to a multimillionaire, or is one of the Rockefeller clan. Look at these bills!" He waved a fistful of restaurant receipts. "And she ate these sumptuous repasts alone! Why alone?" He turned his rage now against me directly.

Instead of paying much attention to Daddy's outburst and, in Gwen's words, his backwoods oratory, my eyes were riveted on Daddy's Masonic order pin, which I believe they call a 32nd-Degree emblem. He always wore this Masonic pin in times of crisis.

My mind also went back to my memory of Daddy's penchant for cuff links. He collected cuff links in the same way I suppose that he had been collecting with Hal Winterrowd his forgotten items. There must have been an entire chiffonier upstairs with his cuff links, cuff links which dated back to the 1860s.

My mind was therefore on his Masonic order pin and his cuff links rather than his acrimonious abuse of me for extravagance.

It was my staring at his Masonic order pin and my knowledge he had a fortune in rare cuff links which prevented my replying to his abuse of me. In order to do something I took out my handkerchief and pretended to blow my nose.

"Anything I can't stand, though, is a weeper." Daddy turned now to Gwen.

"Who is weeping, you ass?" she roared back. "Tell me."

"I say now, and I repeat, anything I can't stand is a woman who snivels," he went on. "How it unnerves a man. My mother would snivel at holy communion when I was a boy. Filled the pew with her tears. I was ashamed, humiliated, lowered my head during the whole service while she streamed and sobbed to her heart's content. Damn such behavior."

"There is nobody sniveling in this room!" Gwen shouted back. "If you had your glasses on, you would know we are all dry-eyed as a sandstorm. And do you know why? Because we know you are a playactor more than you're a man. You missed your calling. You should have been before the footlights. And, as to your miserable wife's expenditures, I applaud her extravagance, do you hear?"

To the amazement, even the disbelief, of both Daddy and me, Gwen now went up to him and removed his Masonic order pin from his lapel, and tossed it down on the little end table.

"A man who rants and raves as you do is not worthy of this emblem, and you know it!" Gwen almost spat out the words.

I forget who stormed out of the room first, Daddy or his sister.

I was left seated in Daddy's armchair, the map of Chicago still in my outstretched hands.

My eyes were dry, my chin was tilted upward, and I knew I was going to be ready for another whirlwind of spending in the "spiffy" restaurants of Chicago's Loop.

❍

But that very evening Daddy paid me a return visit.

With only a faint knock, he opened the door to my room, and asked in an oversweet voice if he could come in.

"Let everything I said to you this afternoon be water under the bridge, Carrie."

He sat down and kept his eyes on the rose carpet, even poking it from time to time with the toe of his high shoe.

"I have been under fearful strain, largely because of Hal's death. I do apologize to you." Here he looked up briefly, and then his eye descended again to the rose carpet.

"You may go to every damned restaurant in the Loop you wish to, so far as I am concerned. If we are ruined financially, let us be ruined, thanks probably in part to Hal Winterrowd. No, of course not. We are not ruined. Not yet. If dining in fancy places gives you a sense of our Gertrude, dine away, dear Carrie. Dine away.

"Allow me to let you in on a little secret, Carrie dear. I was so upset over Hal Winterrowd's demise and the fact that there was no one to carry on the special project of mine that on the spur of the moment I paid a visit to our old friend Evelyn Mae Awbridge."

My look of astonishment only egged Daddy on.

"Well, Carrie dear, you certainly know Evelyn Mae of course. The brilliant professor of Elizabethan English at the university. Friend of our Gertrude, too."

"Of course, I know Evelyn Mae," I spoke up with a loudness and self-assurance more like Gwen than me.

"And you do get along with Evelyn Mae, Carrie, I am sure."

"I've always been very fond of her, you know that." (I was more than puzzled at what he was driving at.)

"She received me with open arms. And, after sharing my concerns over Hal's passing, she pointed out that young as he was Cy Mellerick himself might turn out to be not such a bad stand-in. I was a bit taken aback by this statement but instead of pursuing this drift I changed the subject to our little spat which grew out of my stinginess over your expenditures."

I all but chuckled at his admitting to his stinginess.

"Evelyn Mae," he spoke now almost in a whisper as if

someone would overhear what he was about to divulge. "Evelyn Mae, Carrie, for all her international fame as an authority on Shakespeare and other great writers, may be even more famous for having been a consultant on codes during the War. . . ."

"Codes? Yes," I replied, remembering Gwen's mention of the term.

Daddy looked at me hesitantly, then added in a sort of lullaby-like manner, "Yes, despite, I say, all her recognition here and abroad, Evelyn Mae is a very lonesome lady. She would dearly love for you to keep company with her awhile. Gwen has made me realize you need a change from us. From me, principally. And Carrie, it would give you relief from me and Gwen and our spats. You do need a change, my dearest girl. Don't deny it."

"I had no idea Evelyn Mae was an authority on codes," I said, for all I could think of at that moment was that it was the *Index of Forgotten Items*, after all, and not me which had propelled Daddy into the company of Evelyn Mae herself.

"Oh, forget I told you about her stint in the War Office, why don't you," Daddy said, for he thought that Evelyn Mae's being a code expert had made me not wish to visit her.

"Of course I will be happy to keep Evelyn Mae company," I spoke now like the old Carrie of past times. "And as you say, it will be a change! And I won't be far away after all from you."

"Then it is all arranged," Daddy sighed, and gave the

rose carpet a last nudge with the toe of his shoe. "I'm glad you are agreeing.

"And you will forgive me being cross about the dining out," he inquired, and came over and quickly gave me a peck on my cheek.

"You know you are always forgiven, Daddy," I said, and I watched the door close behind him.

"But, Evelyn Mae," I said aloud. "I wonder do I want to go there. Change, so I need a change! And to think I have carte blanche for the restaurants in the Loop!"

○

I will never forget that hot August day when Evelyn Mae opened the door of her four-story mansion to greet and usher me into her spacious sitting room.

I had no more seated myself than a servant brought me a glass of rather bitter cherry-tasting liquid. It made my eyes smart and open wide.

Evelyn Mae Awbridge, the renowned professor of Elizabethan literature, was perhaps fifty, possibly older, with raven-black straight hair and a large aquiline nose which caused her hazel eyes somehow to appear slightly crossed. Everywhere in the room we were surrounded by, even barricaded with, books reaching from the thick green carpets to the high deadly white ceiling across which gleamed an emblem of enormous embossed chaplet or wreath.

"I can always still see you, dear Carrie," Evelyn Mae began, "as you appeared at one of Gertrude's gallery shows. But with such a crush of people, and you know how I hate gatherings, well, I hardly got to exchange a word with you. Now thanks to Daddy, as you call him, you are here for a visit, and we can talk to our hearts' content."

"Gertrude!" I repeated the name as if Evelyn Mae had mentioned someone going back to my own childhood, so remote all at once did my daughter now seem to me.

I drank more of the cherry liquid.

"Wonderful girl that she was," Evelyn Mae spoke in a whisper.

She came over to me and poured me more of the cherry drink from a pitcher which also contained ice shavings.

"It can't harm you at all, my dear. Not alcoholic. Just fruit and herbs, an old recipe of my own. Drink all you care to.

"I want you to stay with me, Carrie." I heard my hostess going on but now her voice sounded far away and as if proceeding in fact from the hundreds of tomes lining the high walls.

"As I told your husband, I have room after room in this old mansion, enough to sleep fifteen or more people." She laughed as she said this, and her laugh gave me a feeling almost of an electric shock, not painful or threatening, but, like the cherry drink, a restorative.

She took a chair now directly beside me as she went on talking.

"My life work is Edmund Spenser."

"Edmund Spenser," I repeated, for I feared I might be suffering from one of my lapses of attention so worrisome to both Daddy and Gwen.

"The greatest poet in a way we have in our language, Carrie. Author of *The Faerie Queene.* I am in the process of debunking nearly everything men have written about him.

"The same men, my dear, who have, by their incompetent cowardly scholarship deprived us of the real flesh-and-blood Shakespeare. Needless to say, they have not allowed us women scholars to publish the truth about Sir Edmund or for that matter Will Shakespeare. But slowly oh so slowly I am in sight of victory! My research on Edmund Spenser—my life work—has gunpowdered to smithereens all the little men who have written about him before. But you wait till they read what I have to say about the Bard of Avon."

I next felt Evelyn Mae's cool hands arranging a pillow behind my neck.

"Allow me to talk on, precious," Evelyn Mae said. "My chatter will soothe you as much as my cherry herbal. If only it can make you forget old Vic, or, as you insist on calling him, Daddy, for a while. I know what you have been through, my dear. But we won't talk about it. You are here for a change. And change you shall have. My child, you can remain with me as long as you desire. Forever if you say the word."

Whether it was the drink she had given me or Evelyn

Mae's rich contralto voice as she spoke on and on about Edmund Spenser, I had fallen into a half-sleep or drowse by her side on an ample settee.

Evelyn Mae was all at once reading aloud to me from a large volume of poetry. Perhaps it was that rich contralto voice or the fact I understood hardly one word of what she read, the sounds reaching me were as entrancing as music.

For the first time in many years, I felt I was myself again. My body and my troubled mind were both almost at peace.

"I want you to put on this ring," I heard Evelyn Mae say when she had closed the volume of poetry. She held up a ring which she must have just removed from her index finger. (She wore many rings on both her hands.) She placed on my left hand, then, what appeared to be a precious stone.

"But dear Evelyn Mae!"

"Don't thank me, Carrie. Someone must have it. I have more rings than if I were a diamond cutter."

Evelyn Mae looked up now as a grandfather clock chimed the hour.

"This very evening," she informed me, "I am to do a reading from the First Book of *The Faerie Queene.*

"Only a few invited guests will be present, so you need not stand on ceremony or have to greet or talk with the assemblages. But I do require your presence. You shall sit in the first row, with 'occupied' signs surrounding you so that you will be free to devote your full attention to my reading. You may even close your eyes and slumber as I read if you wish. I do feel I require your presence tonight! Stage fright, oh yes. I am as if palsied when I see human eyes gazing at me, and though I have the book of the divine Edmund before me, the terror will not away."

Then, Evelyn Mae rose to her full height. "Until tonight," she smiled, "and if you need anything, you have only to call Alec here."

A young man had entered the room wearing full evening dress, and bowing he led the way to my sleeping room. As I followed Alec down the long hall I felt I had not only left Daddy's modest surroundings but had seen the last of Chicago itself.

I must have slept all the remaining hours of the day until Alec entered my room carrying a tray with a king-size cup of steaming liquid.

"This will tide you over, ma'am, until late supper," he spoke encouragingly. The drink gave off an aroma something like bouillon. Tiny little wheaten stars were swimming in it.

I drank it down almost at a swallow.

"Miss Awbridge also wishes you would wear this gown for the reading if you please," Alec said and pointed to a chair on which hung a dress trimmed with embroidered gold lace and sparkling lamé. A wave of disbelief and strong incredulity crept over me. I could scarcely believe what was happening *was* happening.

Seeing me hesitate, Alec went on to say that Miss Awbridge will be more than satisfied if you also will keep the gown for your very own.

Evelyn Mae was already at the podium when I entered her recital room. She was wearing an evening dress of black velvet with sable and pink silk, and cerise trim. A massive crucifix hung almost to her waist.

She was looking fiercely about the room, but when she caught sight of me she beamed and nodded and pointed to the chair in the first row.

My gaze was distracted from the podium, however, by the sight of a bevy of young men who had begun to fill the room to capacity. They looked almost ridiculously young for such an occasion and all were wearing evening clothes of a cut too large for them and of a style which belonged to another age and time. They all sat as if immobilized, their eyes fixed on Evelyn Mae who it seemed clear was their idol.

The lights of the room were dimming and after sipping from a cup very much like the one Alec had handed me in my sleeping room, Evelyn Mae was about to begin her reading when the door to the recital room opened abruptly and noisily and Daddy entered.

In the dimness of the room he stumbled badly and one heard him swear loudly.

Daddy staggered into the chair beside me although there was a large card with the words RESERVED across it.

Daddy grasped my hand tightly and mumbled a few phrases.

Evelyn Mae had now put on enormous sparkling spectacles and in a voice which needed no amplification she had begun her recital from *The Faerie Queene.*

Daddy as if he were alone with me on Stony Island Avenue began kissing my left hand again and again.

Out of the corner of my eye I watched Daddy stare at the gown I was wearing, and he gave a long suspicious look at the ring on my finger. He tried to say something several times, but the voice of Evelyn Mae drowned out all other sounds.

At the end of her recitation there came a storm of applause from the young men who standing shouted, "Brava."

Several bouquets of roses and tropical lilies were bought to the podium and Evelyn Mae bowed almost to the ground.

Then I heard Daddy say, "Carrie, tell me, have I done the right thing? Are you, dear, going to be all right here. I dare say it is a change, but is it the right change, do you think?"

"It's certainly a far cry from Stony Island Avenue, isn't it, Daddy?"

He shook his head gravely as he took in again the ring with the precious gem and the regal gown Evelyn Mae had given me.

We were now ushered into the mammoth dining room, but neither Daddy nor I had any appetite, and we sat a good deal away from the diners who stood eating about the long table heavy with guinea hen under glass, sides of

beef, piles of paprika-sprinkled mashed potatoes, and plat-
ters of exotic vegetables whose names I never knew.

"You are not fasting!" We heard the voice of Evelyn Mae.

"You'll excuse us, Evelyn Mae," Daddy spoke up. "It's
a bit late for us old folks to dine, if I may say so." Rising
slowly, Daddy said a few words of praise for the reading,
then added somewhat bashfully, "Evelyn Mae, these
young men unless I am mistaken are all star football players on the Varsity Team."

Evelyn Mae beamed and nodded.

"I must have a private word with your husband," our
hostess now turned to me. "Right over here," she ushered
Daddy to a kind of private nook in the dining hall, where
I watched them nervously as they began their private chat.
I saw Evelyn Mae had taken on a somewhat dour expres-
sion as she appeared in a disputatious frame of mind.

As their confab, to borrow one of Daddy's own favorite
expressions, appeared to be rather lengthy, one of the
young football players brought me a plate of roast goose
and truffles and more to please him than anything else I
managed to take a few bites.

Finally Evelyn Mae and Daddy came back to where I
was seated.

"Dear Dr. Awbridge has prevailed upon me to let you
stay, Carrie." Daddy spoke to me in a hoarse voice. "And
for just as long a time as you care to!"

"One would think you were sending her off on a dirigi-
ble," Evelyn Mae remarked. She was moving a palm-leaf
fan against her face swimming with perspiration.

I could see that Daddy was loath to leave me, but Evelyn Mae took him by the arm and led him away into the next room from where she said her good-byes at the main door.

I could not help myself. Without ceremony I left Evelyn Mae's side and rushed to the front window, where I saw Daddy angrily take out from his breast pocket a Havana cigar, bite off the end and spit it out and then, with a cigarette lighter I had never seen before, he angrily lit his smoke. I could not hear the words he let loose, but I knew they were his strongest profanity.

All at once, I thought I could hear in my mind's eye the words from the poem Evelyn Mae had been reciting as clear as if Evelyn Mae herself was reciting it only for me:

> *My love is now awake out of her dream*
> *And her fair eyes like stars that dimmèd were*
> *with darksome cloud, now show their goodly beams!*

Turning around I saw Evelyn Mae herself smiling and beckoning me to follow her back to the front parlor.

Almost as in something one daydreams, I found myself sitting with Evelyn Mae on a horsehair sofa. Occasionally she would smooth my hair and gently rub my neck, for she knew I often complained of headache.

"Daddy"—she used my name for him now—"and I have had a good chat about you," she began. "He feels terribly guilty with regard to you, Carrie. Claims though he has always acted in good faith and for your own good. I let him believe that."

I don't think I ever told Evelyn Mae how much I had pitied Daddy the evening he came unannounced at the poetry reading, that I suffered too seeing him defending himself against her greater poise and strength.

A strange phrase kept coming into my head, perhaps issuing from the poetry I had heard.

Your formal life has come to an end! Those were the words, like the cadences of Spenser, which recurred to me again and again.

"There is something I have never told you," Evelyn Mae took one of my hands in hers and patted it gently. "Oh, perhaps I should not mention it. No matter then. Gertrude in her last days was often a visitor here, but you know that. Very near the end she took me into her confidence."

"You were close to Gertrude?" I wondered uneasily.

Evelyn Mae rose now and began walking around the room. I feared for a moment she might be going to read again from *The Faerie Queene*.

"Not exactly close. Gertrude, however," she went on, "asked if I would look after you when she was gone."

I closed both my eyes tight.

"You know of course what my answer was, Carrie. I promised your daughter I would, but until now I am afraid I have not kept my promise.

"Do you know who you remind me of, Carrie," she said after a lengthy pause.

"I will tell you," she said.

"*Demeter*," she spoke in a voice so low I was not sure I heard her.

Impatient because she felt I did not know who Demeter was, she added, "The goddess Ceres, the Earth mother who lost her daughter *Persephone* to the King of the Under-world. You know the story."

I pretended I did.

"You, like her, have lost the most precious thing in your life. How can any man understand the love of a mother for her daughter? How can any man understand anything about a woman?" She raised her hand at that moment as if she feared I would interrupt or contradict her.

"Is there any ill or sorrow that men have not bestowed on us women? There is none." She came close to shouting the last sentence.

"Yes," she mused, sitting down and daubing her eyes now with a handkerchief she drew from her bosom. "They inhabit an entirely different sphere. They would regard Demeter as a madwoman. They would tell her to forget her Persephone. But you, dear child, were robbed of Gertrude almost from the time she was born."

I nodded dispiritedly.

"And so you want to find some bits and pieces of your darling, late as it is," she gave me an eloquent look.

"And though Daddy in our private talk tonight wishes you to return to him within a day or two, you may as far as I am concerned, stay here with me for so long as you choose. You must regard my house as your own, Carrie."

It was my turn now to take Evelyn Mae's hand in mine.

"Daddy is as you know nearly beside himself over the death of Hal Winterrowd. I thought it impolite to tell him that Hal Winterrowd hardly spent ten minutes a year on Daddy's account with him. Someone else has been doing yeoman's service there!"

Seeing I did not know who this someone was, she went on.

"Young Cy Mellerick has been doing all the work old Hal was supposed to have done."

"Cy Mellerick! Wasn't he the same young man who was a friend of Gertrude?"

She nodded.

"May I tell you something in strictest confidence, Carrie. Cy Mellerick in the law office on La Salle Street has not only been busy with columns of figures and real estate receipts. Though he is perfectly competent to handle those matters. No, he has also been occupied by another matter."

"Is it the *Index of Forgotten Items?*" I blurted out.

Had I thrown a glass of ice water in my friend's face she could not have been taken more aback.

"But did Daddy reveal this secret of his to you?"

"I'm afraid not," I said, and I stood up hurriedly.

"Carrie, will you please sit down. See how rattled I am with what you have let out of the bag."

I remained standing as I explained how I went to Daddy's den in search of more private ledgers Gertrude may have left behind. And which Daddy did not want me to see. "Yes," my voice almost broke. "So, I have been indiscreet. And then having come across the *Index of Forgotten Items,* I began reading them. My sister-in-law entered as I was reading away."

"God alive," Evelyn Mae whispered, and then burst out laughing. "Old Gwendolyn caught you red-handed."

I wanted to cry rather than laugh, I felt so discomfited.

"And you read these pages Daddy has written over the years?"

"Yes, and had they been in Ancient Egyptian I would have been just as knowledgeable about what Daddy had written down there."

"But you must have recognized some of the people and events he has bothered to record."

"Oh well, there are countless lists, such as heavyweight champions of the ring, baseball greats and matinee idols. But apropos of what?"

"And Gwen is in on this with you?"

"No, no," I was vociferous.

"I may as well tell you that your sister-in-law is also occupied with a mysterious task. She had come to me for advice on that score time and again."

"Do you mean Nettie Smith and the son of the Tiger of France."

"Carrie, Carrie," Evelyn Mae grinned. "So contrary to what people say about you, you do know everything."

"And Cy Mellerick of course knew my daughter, didn't he?" I changed back to a subject which was more closer to me than mysterious ledgers and scandalous marriages.

"Carrie," Evelyn Mae spoke now in a more grave and professional manner, "I think we have said enough tonight about these matters."

She remained silent for an awkward space.

I remembered a remark my mother had often made in the face of difficulties: It will all come out in Monday's wash.

I thought then that the mysteries we were talking about would never come out for me to understand—ever!

By this time the gala had come to a slow majestic end and Evelyn Mae held my arm gently as we went up the long staircase to our sleeping quarters.

Before she bid me good night, Evelyn Mae took my two hands in hers and kissed the tips of my fingers. As she left me I caught coming from her touch a kind of fragrance I had never experienced before. For the first time in my life, I felt if not happy, at peace.

❖

Whether it was Daddy's sudden and unexpected appearance, or the overstimulation of the gala reading itself, I found sleep that night impossible. And even when I dozed off for a few minutes, I would be dreaming of Daddy and Evelyn Mae and of the shadowy figure of Edmund Spenser.

The phrase I had heard that evening, *the end of your formal life,* also recurred again and again like something amplified repeatedly from a distant chamber.

Waking from time to time I wondered if perhaps I had

died and was in some remote after-world. And that Evelyn Mae, like me, was one of the "passed over" ones.

Then, too, would begin in recollection her tirade against the breed of men, as she would condemn the race of males from the day of Adam down to the present occupant of the White House (she called him the white crocodile). Under the remembrance of her outbursts I came to the realization that I had perhaps never known any men. For now it seemed that Daddy himself was only a simulacrum of a man, not a flesh-and-blood husband.

What on earth would Gertrude have thought had she known I sat hour after hour hearing this learned doctor of letters read to me from a book of cantos by Spenser. Yes, I, whom Gertrude had often thrown up to that I had never read an entire book from cover to cover, or a remark I overheard her make to one of her lovers, "My mother is as unsophisticated as the woman who takes in our washing."

And again in broken slumber I would have sworn I heard Evelyn Mae's voice saying, "Do you know, my dear Carrie, that Edmund"—she meant of course the poet of *The Faerie Queene*—"died in what we would call today a flophouse, practically starving to death, forgotten by everyone except a handful of other indigent lost persons, and so he suffered a derelict's death in King Street Westminster. I would have given my own life to have rescued him!" She choked out the words.

After this dream came more dreams. I thought that Daddy had summoned me and warned me against Evelyn Mae with the words: "She only knows what she has read, and she has read too much. A purblind old cat. I have had her number from time immemorial! I forbid you to see her," I thought I heard him in my sleep. "I am ordering you to leave her house on the grounds she is a deleterious influence on you. Listen to me, Carrie, you cannot, you must not desert my bed and board. Not after forty years!" I then remembered Evelyn Mae's dictum. "Contrary to what everybody says about you, Carrie dear, you know everything." But it was untrue. It was Evelyn Mae who knew everything. Didn't she know of *The Forgotten Items* before Daddy had visited her. How long had she known about Gwen's friendship with Nettie Smith and her supposed marriage to the Tiger of France's son? How much did she know about Gertrude? About Cy Mellerick? Yes, Daddy, it's been "forty years" of being kept in the dark about everything. And only when you are forced to tell me do I hear one word from you!

I raised up in bed, for I was certain Daddy was in my sleeping chamber ordering me to come home to him.

"No," I addressed the empty air of the room, "I am staying with Evelyn Mae, till the coast is clear."

"The coast?" Daddy spat out the word with utter disgust. "The coast be damned! You are coming home with me this instant."

○

How I welcomed the morning light after those long hours and their afflicting nightmares.

Evelyn Mae was waiting for me in what she called her Crocus Room where we took breakfast.

"I want you to come with me to my upstairs apparel room for a look about," she said once we had breakfasted. "And let's get out what the sandman has left in your eyes."

One of Evelyn Mae's most costly hobbies, I learned this now hardly to my surprise, was her collection of hats. A whole room of hats—enough hats to open a millinery shop with. But more than the hats, it was the hat pins which were her pride and joy.

"May I look at them, dear friend?"

"You need never ask," she led me up to an otherwise vacant room.

She raised the heavy blind over an arched window.

"Look your fill!"

She sat down in a heavy chair as I picked up one hat after another, taking each one from its little cubicle. Yes, they were all arranged like precious manuscripts. Evelyn Mae told me that trying on one hat after another often helped her solve a problem or at least put her in a better mood.

But it was the hat pins I was drawn to. The sparkling kind of glass especially in the ornamented heads of the pins.

They appeared to be, these ornamented heads, like precious jewels. Rubies, opals, emeralds, garnets and more!

From her chair Evelyn Mae smiled and nodded.

"Collected over a lifetime," she informed me.

"And you wear them all?"

"Almost all, Carrie dear."

I was so overcome by such extravagant display that,

seeing there was no other chair in the room except for the one my friend sat in, I slipped down to sit on the floor still gazing at the collection of the hats.

Meanwhile Alec entered the room and served us tea.

Evelyn Mae and I drank one cup after another, she seated on her throne chair and I, yes, still sitting on the floor on her Turkey carpet, looking up all the while at the ornamented heads of the effulgent hats.

To please me now Evelyn Mae rose and put on one of her hats having a small plume on the back and walked up and down the room. Not only did her strolling about as she put on one hat after another soothe and delight me, it brought a becoming flush to Evelyn Mae's usually pallid cheeks. Her eyes also began to shine like the glass of the ornamented heads of the pins.

Yes, I believe at that moment I was almost happy! But I lived also in a vague dread that she would tire of me and send me back to Daddy.

○

A few days later my absence from Daddy began to pall on me. Evelyn Mae was the first to notice my absentmindedness.

"There's something troubling you," she remarked one evening after we had been entertained by some of her young musicians. "Tell me, Carrie, is there anything you are in need of? What have I overlooked for your needs?"

"You have given me more than anybody could possibly require, you must know that."

Evelyn Mae shook her head gravely for she knew perfectly well what was troubling me.

Tossing and turning that night, I finally gave up thinking even of sleeping. All at once, without realizing what I was doing, I put on my clothes and shoes.

I was desperately homesick for Daddy. I felt at that moment if I did not see him I would collapse with sorrow.

I walked out of Evelyn Mae's house without realizing it was three o'clock in the morning.

After some little struggle with my own key I opened the front door and walked upstairs to his sleeping room.

Like me Daddy was a light sleeper and I found him in bed reading, I suppose, from his ten thousand pages.

He was too astonished to speak for a moment.

Instead of greeting me Daddy gave me the news that Gwen had gone back to Paris. "Until the next time," he added.

"Oh, Daddy," was all I could say and I sat down in a small rocking chair facing the bed.

"What on earth do I owe this visit for," he wondered.

"I should never have left you, Daddy. Who is by the way taking care of you."

"You know Maud's older daughter? She looks in on me frequently."

"And so Gwen has washed her hands of us." I went back to the news of my sister-in-law.

"Listen, Carrie," Daddy got out of bed now and put on his carpet slippers. "You desperately needed a change. I knew Gwen was getting on your nerves. I don't need to mention my nerves. So stick it out with Evelyn Mae, dear girl, why don't you? I was too much for you."

"You were not, Daddy, you were not.

"Oh, I don't know what's wrong with me, Daddy. I love Evelyn Mae. If anything she is too good to me. She's overwhelmed me with kindness."

"Stick it out, Carrie."

"Don't you want me back?"

"More than anything in the world. But I also want you to remain in the land of the living. Evelyn Mae is your tonic. After a while you will come home or I hope so."

"How can you doubt that? I'm ready to come home now."

"Carrie, thank my lucky stars you dropped in on me tonight. Makes me believe in telepathy. I am still not over what occurred a few hours ago."

The expression on my face must have disturbed Daddy for he said, "Oh, it's nothing that godawful, sweetheart. But I've had a visitor tonight. A visitor I never dreamed to lay eyes on for that matter."

He kept dawdling and his wasting time like this frightened me.

"Imagine, young Cy Mellerick showed up here. Must have been midnight. I have only seen him once or twice on the few times I went to La Salle Street to talk with old Hal. I barely knew Cy was his assistant, but the way Hal talked I didn't think Cy did more than hold Hal's coat when he left for the night, or maybe mailed letters. Now I know different!"

Daddy rose now and went to one of his filing cabinets and drew out a few letters.

Sitting down again he went on. "It must have been devilish hard for young Cy to tell me what he told me. I think he called it making a clean breast of it all.

"I don't think you ever met or knew this young Mellerick very well, isn't that a fact."

I hardly dared say one word in reply and Daddy went on talking.

"He's a handsome boy come to think of it. His brother was a war hero.

"Cy said that talking with me was like talking with his brother. Especially when it had to do with the important matter on his mind."

"And what was that important matter," I wondered, but Daddy did not hear me.

"This is what he told me," and Daddy shook his head as if it was either the worst news anybody had handed him, or the most unbelievable, or maybe both.

"I told both you and Gwen that I had been working on a project of mine I called *The Forgotten Items.* Just random jottings, comments, reminiscences, of no interest to anybody but me, I suppose. Still I had been at work on it for thirty years. It needed some sorting through and perhaps recopying here and there. And Hal Winterrowd was at the beginning the only person who knew of the existence of my *Items.* Him and me. Nobody else.

"Now young Cy tells me this. Hal Winterrowd hardly ever peeped into all those ten or twenty thousand pages. Did nothing with them. So young Cy swears and I believe him. There sat all those pages untended, unread, uncared for. Ignored. Might as well have been truly forgotten themselves. But young Cy read them, again and again, almost memorized them. He began to sort them out, put them in order. Rearranged the order. God knows what all. By this time Hal Winterrowd was so far gone he hardly remembered that my *Items* existed.

"So all these years it was Cy and not Hal who was doing yeoman's service.

"I saw, of course, Cy was in awe of me as he had been in awe of his war-hero brother. How was he to tell me he was the only one outside of myself who knew of the existence of my ten thousand pages, had read and reread them? Understood and prized them, so he says, perhaps more than me even. But not quite of course.

"So what he calls the zero hour arrived. He had to come to tell me. I think he thought I was going to prosecute him. Prosecute someone who loved, believed and cherished my *Items*!

"But I was so astonished by his confession I was speechless for a good five minutes and then I saw he was getting up to leave.

" 'For God's sake sit down,' I told him.

" 'I apologize,' he said.

" 'Apologize,' I said, 'Christ in Heaven, for what? For

saving my *Items*. Damn it to hell, don't dare leave. You are a man after my own heart.'

"I brought out my oldest bourbon and we drank temperately for I saw the poor chap didn't care for strong drink.

" 'You are unaware of what you have done for me,' I told him. 'You have performed a strange miracle. Only you have read them, only you have been tending to them, only you am I beholden to.'

"We laughed, then we chuckled. We even sort of sobbed and bawled.

" 'You have brought me back from No Man's Land, Cy Mellerick, and you didn't know what you have done. You don't know you have miracles in your fingers. How can I thank you?' Then all at once out of the blue he said, 'I knew Gertrude very well.'

"For a minute I didn't know who he meant. It was so hard for me to associate a young man like Cy who had rescued my *Items* with someone who had been close to my daughter. They seemed at that moment worlds apart.

" 'You were close to her,' I gasped.

"He nodded and tried to taste more of the bourbon.

" 'My wife will want to know,' I told him."

"Thank God," I cried.

"Thank God for what," Daddy said in his old crosspatch manner.

"Thank God he knew our daughter," I cried, for I was nearly bawling too. "Maybe he can talk to me about her."

Daddy nodded again and half smiled.

"Anyone who could save my *Items* from dusty oblivion can surely talk to you about our Gertrude. Why not. Why not get him to talk to you about her or anything else. We have to be careful not to lose such a young man, wouldn't you say."

I felt at that moment all the weight of all those ten thousand pages had been lifted from my own shoulders.

"Carrie, oh, Carrie," he cried as I rose to leave and go back to Evelyn Mae.

"Carrie, your search of Gertrude must be something like my compiling *The Forgotten Items*."

"Oh, I may never find what I'm looking for in Gertrude. I know that."

"But Evelyn Mae is right, you should get it out of your system."

"What a peculiar term for my search.

"Oh, Daddy, I am such a failure at everything."

I longed to be able to burst into tears at that moment.

Those lovable looks Daddy gave me nearly finished me.

"All right then, let me go back to Evelyn Mae's," I managed to say.

"I won't drive you out of our home, Carrie."

"Perhaps you don't need me now there's Maud's daughter."

"Nothing of the kind. I want you to feel what the change is doing for you. For, Carrie, you look refreshed and younger since you went to Evelyn Mae's. Give it a little more time. Then come back to me."

"Daddy, Daddy," was all I could say. I turned, then

without another word walked down the staircase and closed the front door behind me.

○

I don't know whether it was Daddy or Evelyn Mae who called me a *pilgrim*. My memory at times seems to be failing me. But once the word *pilgrim* began going round and round in my mind I saw it was I suppose true. True that I was a pilgrim.

What hurt me to the quick though was that Daddy did not want me to stay with him. I wondered if anyone might be taking my place. And then I realized that I was sorry Gwen had decamped. For all of the misery she had caused me I missed her. Even wanted her back. I felt I would never see her again.

I was lonesome for Daddy and Gwen.

And I was still heartsick over the fact that all these years Daddy had never said boo about his secret either.

I tried to summarize our speaking together in the dead of night.

I was to go on searching for Gertrude with Cy Mellerick as my approved guide, and for now I was to let Daddy alone.

And so I came back to Evelyn Mae's with, as Daddy would say, my tail between my legs.

She beamed at me over the breakfast table. She must have felt something was amiss.

She took my head in her arms and kissed my forehead and smoothed my hair.

"We have made a great deal of progress."

"Was it you who called me a *pilgrim,*" I interrupted her.

"I, child?" She seemed not to remember.

"I must have dreamed it," I mumbled.

◦

In the next few days Evelyn Mae's domicile became even more animated and bustling perhaps than the Chicago Opera. Men of all ages were everywhere, indeed as if they were part of some rehearsal for a very grand theater piece. And from one of the distant rooms above I heard the sound of oboes, clarinets and saxophones, and the thundering preeminence of a player piano repeating the same solo piece constantly.

All this splendor brought home to me the drab, home-spun, seedy life I had lived with Daddy, and a kind of crack in my own perception of the world gave me at least the beginning of my understanding of why Gertrude had left and renounced me. It was not so much my failing as a mother, for I had always dimly known how completely I had failed her there, but Gertrude approaching woman-hood could no longer endure the sapless, the airless, the faded, the dowdy gentility of Stony Island Avenue. She had left us so that, as her Record Book put it, she wouldn't turn to stone or be a poor fluttering fly in a deserted spider's web.

The next day as if she understood my being so at sea, Evelyn Mae (she never missed a thing!) approached me now. Sitting down beside me, she took my hand in hers and then to my surprised and unabashed pleasure she kissed all the fingers of my right hand.

"Let me take you for a drive in my Electric," she said.

"My motorcar," she repeated when she saw I did not register what she meant.

Seated in this strange vehicle and watching with astonishment as Evelyn Mae grasped a long black rod which was what drove the antique car forward and backwards, I saw passing by us my own neighborhood in as different a light as if my friend and I were in an airborne balloon.

She stopped her Electric at last once in front of a decayed row of barn-like cottages on Fifty-seventh Street which Evelyn Mae pointed out were built during the World's Columbian Exposition of 1893.

"And here"—she turned to look me square in the eyes—"your Gertrude painted some of her best portraits."

She shook her head. I knew what Evelyn Mae was thinking, that I had never visited Gertrude in one of those forlorn shacks where she created her masterpieces.

We drove on and on and Evelyn Mae would point out from time to time other residences in which Gertrude had painted her now famous work. I was shamefaced when Evelyn Mae had to awaken me, for the smooth ride in the Electric car had caused me to fall into a heavy slumber.

"To think, Carrie," she said as we drove back to her mansion, "our city known today as the Gem of the Prairies was once a savage wilderness of dripping wet grass and mud flats, alongside the Great Lake which itself was once only a lonely silent wasteland."

Coming home after our ride in the Electric, we saw Alec approach with an anxious ruffled expression.

"A Mr. Cy Mellerick, ma'am, is waiting in the sitting room to see Miss Carrie."

"Cy Mellerick?" Evelyn Mae spoke in some confusion for her. She gave a wondering look in my direction.

"Ah, yes," my voice faltered, "yes, Evelyn Mae, Daddy told me that Cy Mellerick might be in touch with me."

For the first time I saw a flash of real temper in Evelyn Mae's face, followed by an expression of deep hurt and disappointment.

But in her old regal manner then Evelyn Mae led me into the waiting room.

Cy Mellerick in all his glory advanced to meet us.

I looked up but instead of seeing Cy Mellerick I thought I beheld Mead Thomas. The man who had entered my line of vision was of course the young attorney.

Both Evelyn Mae and Cy Mellerick were aware of my confusion.

I managed to get out a few monosyllables and extended my hand to Cy.

To add to my further discomfiture, I saw that Evelyn Mae was rattled.

Cy Mellerick himself stood unperturbed and tall. (Tall and winsome as Hermes, Evelyn Mae would later describe him.)

Then we were all seated at last and I could take in his curly hair, his eyes almost violet in color with huge pupils, and eyelashes which appeared to sweep down upon his cheeks, and then the scar around his mouth or rather two white scars which somehow only brought out the more his handsomeness.

Evelyn Mae started right in, "Gertrude had many admirers, many followers, but not one of them could hold a candle to you, Cy Mellerick."

I was a bit taken aback at this statement. And I saw that Cy Mellerick, too, had blushed deeply. I was becoming so flustered and uneasy at the appearance of our young visitor that I was hardly hearing a word Evelyn Mae was speaking.

"But for the present," she chimed in at some point, "Carrie would be very interested in hearing about your custody of *The Forgotten Items.*"

Cy Mellerick fidgeted now, and as he did so I recalled Daddy having told me Cy had been wounded in the war. I gave a quick glance again at the scars around his mouth and chin.

"It's no longer a secret," Evelyn Mae was going on. "Carrie discovered Daddy's *Forgotten Items* by chance."

"Daddy, yes." Cy Mellerick indicated he knew my name for my husband.

I thought for a moment Evelyn Mae had blushed! But it was only a moving of the sunlight at that moment across her face. Some time later, without my hardly noticing it, I became aware that Evelyn Mae had taken her leave of us. I was now at the mercy of my own shyness and awkwardness.

Cy Mellerick was speaking now, "Your husband told me you would appreciate anything at all I may remember of my friendship with your daughter, Gertrude."

A strained long silence ensued.

"I told your husband that it would be fine with me. That I would be more than happy to oblige."

Having said this he crossed and recrossed his legs. The scars on his face appeared whiter then, or was it the sun reaching him now.

"Of course," he thought back, "there were others who knew more about such a great painter."

"Others," I wondered in a voice which boomed loudly.

"As a matter of fact, there is almost no one of my age still hereabouts who knew Gertrude."

Cy, I realized then, had handed me his card with several phone numbers, one of which, underlined in red, was a private wire.

○

A few hours after Cy had left us, as we were sipping yet another blend of Evelyn Mae's special tea I blurted out, "What has Daddy done?" I spoke this more to myself than to her.

"Brought two desperate persons together. Don't you see you are to be friends?"

"Friends," I repeated and Evelyn Mae gave me a curious all-knowing look.

"You can't believe what you say, that I care more for this young attorney than for you."

"But you do," she smoothed my hair and pulled a little on one of my ear lobes. "I suppose one can call it chance, isn't everything that, and I know you care for me."

"Care for you! You have saved me, don't you see. I could no longer breathe under the same roof with Daddy. You know that! Don't make me leave you. Whatever you do. Shut me up if you must in some attic room without windows, don't make me go back, not yet."

"You can only say that, Carrie, because you have met him."

"I know you too well to believe you are mocking me," I mumbled.

"You have never understood yourself. You have lived your life not to understand yourself. But as so often happens, you have met a force which if you want to call it blind, do so, a force which will make you love him and make him love you."

I touched the hem of her long green silk dress, and she went on smoothing my hair and kissing me from time to time as she had never done before.

"Your sister-in-law," Evelyn Mae began, "Gwen, told me she could never believe you once sang in the chorus of the Chicago Opera. But do you know what, Carrie, after your meeting with Cy Mellerick I can see that you did sing in the opera after all. Even if only for a short season. I see you differently now than you see yourself."

I lay in the dark in my room going over and over in my mind what Evelyn Mae had told me—that I was taken with Cy Mellerick, and that Evelyn Mae herself loved me.

Living with Daddy I had been reminded constantly of what my mother had called her own declining years— going down the *shady path of life.*

Now all at once I had left the security and quiet of Daddy to be dazzled, bewildered, and driven beside myself under the tutelage of the most overpowering human being I had ever met, Evelyn Mae. I felt I could be losing my own willpower and direction. But I could almost hear my hostess's rejoinder to this thought of mine, "When did you have your own willpower or individual freedom living with Daddy, will you tell me that."

And furthermore (I went over my predicament) Daddy himself had palmed me off on Evelyn Mae! And she had told me time and again that I could stay with her forever, be loved by her forever.

Now however, the coming of Cy Mellerick into my life had made even Evelyn Mae and her mansion of so many rooms only a temporary residence for me. And should I return to Daddy? Indeed did Daddy wish me to return? Perhaps his mind was poisoned by Gwendolyn.

But how could I, walking down the *shady path of life,* be taken by a young man like Cy Mellerick or even more important how could he love me?

"You seem to have a very narrow definition of love." Evelyn Mae was speaking to me in her sitting room with the blinds drawn and somewhere from one of her upper stories something very much like a player piano was going.

"I'm afraid, Evelyn Mae, nothing I think, none of my ideas can hold a candle to a woman of your intellect."

"Poppycock," she shot back. "Everyone has their own authenticity."

I often wondered back then who would believe my story if I should put it all down in the way Daddy and Gertrude had confined their secret thoughts and feelings to Record Books and *Forgotten Items*.

Daddy, as I have said so many times, seemed to have washed his hands of me and given the burden of caring for me to Evelyn Mae. Evelyn Mae in turn, despite her ardent protestations of love and sympathy was, I felt, wishing for Cy Mellerick to take me in charge—at least for a while.

She claimed time and again that she could see the "love light" in my eyes whenever Cy Mellerick appeared at her mansion.

She again compared him to the Greek Hermes leading me through the dark passages of the world in search of my lost daughter.

I could see perfectly well that Cy Mellerick had been commissioned to take me in hand.

Cy and I followed some of the route covered by Evelyn Mae in her Electric.

Cy and I, however, walked down Fifty-seventh Street and Dorchester Avenue so that he could point out to me the "haunts" of Gertrude. He also took me to the pool parlors and bowling alleys where she found many admirers.

He then confided in me a fact which took me by complete surprise.

Gertrude had left to Cy Mellerick her main studio which occupied two top floors of an old brownstone in bad repair, inhabited now only by her paintings.

"You will have to give me time before we go there," I told him.

He made an attempt to smile and I again noticed the scars about his mouth and chin and for the first time— since we were now walking—I realized there was something wrong with one of his legs for he limped. I recalled someone telling me he had been badly wounded in the war.

It also dawned on me that perhaps Cy Mellerick too was looking for someone on whom he could rely or, perhaps a better word, lean.

○

"So the cat is out of the bag!"

Cy Mellerick's vibrant voice brought me to full attention.

We were seated on a bench in Jackson Park, not too

far from the lake. Several minutes had passed in comfortable silence since his words about Daddy's discovery
that it was Cy and not Hal who had been acting in his
behalf. "Yes," he went on, "it must have been a hard
thing to swallow.

"And he has taken it in stride," Cy continued, telling of
his meeting with Daddy, and that Daddy was resigned to
Cy's place in his life.

"Since he is over the shock and the surprise," Cy
added giggling.

Every time I was with the young attorney I was surprised all over again by his youth, for youth he appeared
to me. How, I wondered, could so young a man be dealing
in the mysteries, confusion and obscurities of anyone like
my husband.

"Then there is Daddy's thanklessness," I practically
heard myself say.

Cy looked at me quizzically.

"Daddy never thanks anyone," I explained. "Especially
those closest to him. So when you see him, don't expect thanks.
Be grateful if you escape without a daily bawling out."

Cy smiled and in that smile I saw he was more strong
than young.

"And he's made it clear, Mrs. Kinsella," he was saying
as my attention was straying to a vendor of balloons for
children. "Your husband wants me to guide you around."

I nodded.

"I still feel I'm afraid a little like a conspirator, Cy," I
tried to explain my dourness.

Oh, how I wanted to tell him of how at sea I was, first by leaving Daddy's home and staying with Evelyn Mae, and now with Daddy's full encouragement being guided about by a young man, yes young enough to be my grandson.

I wanted to tell him then that I was lost. That I had been removed from my place with Daddy, somehow.

"But our purpose, dear Carrie"—I now came back from my woolgathering to hear what my guide was saying—"our purpose according to Daddy, if I may call him that, is this: We are to search out the real Gertrude.

"And lo and behold Mrs. Kinsella, let me tell you"—and here he struck his hand against the bench we were seated on—"for here, yes, right here, we are seated on the very bench, yes the very weatherbeaten bench on which your daughter and I spent so many endless hours."

He clicked his tongue and shook his head.

I stared at him. I stared at the bench.

"I think I, too, have my own *Forgotten Items*," he went on, "only they're all in my head, not written down. I've never shared them with anybody except maybe Gertrude. The funny thing though, Carrie"—he lingered awkwardly over my first name—"I have the feeling I might let you hear them. They might come out of me someday all at once as we go on seeing one another."

He gazed then toward the interior of the park in a manner that made me feel he had left me and was perhaps back to his times with Gertrude.

❍

Several days later we were walking in this direction. Indeed I wondered where Cy was taking me. We had plunged all at once into a section of the park I never knew existed. The terrain became difficult and Cy several times held my hand.

"We are going to the 'grottoes,' " he informed me.

My bewildered look made him laugh.

"Even people," he said, "who have lived all their lives in this neighborhood don't know of the existence of the 'grottoes.' "

"Certainly I don't," I muttered.

The path we were on now took a steep declivity. "It was her favorite place. She once told me she wouldn't mind living here."

"But what on earth kind of place is it?"

Our descent on the path which was overgrown with every kind of vegetation and the roots of old trees gave me the impression we were going as Evelyn Mae might have said to *terra incognita.*

Then the path ended and we stood before the *grottoes* themselves.

It must have been at one time, I thought, a huge banquet hall or refectory dating from the last century. The building was now in ruins and the roof itself appeared to be in a final state of collapse.

"And this was her favorite place!" I could not conceal my sorrow.

"Her favorite-favorite place!" he almost shouted. "It's probably too dangerous to actually go inside," Cy remarked. So rather than enter the building we sat on the front steps and looked in.

"Her favorite-favorite place!" I echoed him.

The wind was up from the lake and made the building rattle and shake.

I began to shiver from the cold and damp. Before I knew it he had helped me into his jacket.

"Here, she told me, in this place spurned by all decent and respectable people, she liked to come with her young men to indulge in forbidden reveries. And gather inspiration for the paintings to come. A ruined building like this was her palace."

"So you mean she came here just to dream."

"No, she came here for everything."

All at once I moved both my hands helplessly. I felt a bit unwell. I felt indeed like I had once as a small girl riding the merry-go-round for the first time and the sight of all the people, trees, and the Ferris wheel rushing past gave me a kind of vertigo.

I reached in my purse for my smelling salts and took a deep whiff. Cy's eye had caught sight of the long tangled trellises of wild, unrestrained vegetation gradually taking over what remained of the *grottoes.* He did not show any interest in the smelling salts and I put them back in my purse.

I was thankful then that I kept a bottle of smelling salts

handy or, as *The Forgotten Items* would have probably called it, the Smelling Bottle.

We sat on in silence for such a long time that I wondered if I had the strength to rise.

I had the definite impression that we were sinking with the *grottoes* deeper into the earth and into past time.

It was then that I realized that he and I would never again be strangers.

His open palm was stretched out as if he was waiting for me to see it.

This brought me again back to my own early youth when along with a classmate of mine, we had taken up palm reading as a hobby.

Both Daddy and, to a certain extent, Gertrude had always derided my interest in what Daddy called occult nonsense.

But seeing Cy's hand—and why did he open up his palm to me there in that desolate place as if he expected me to read the message of its lines.

"What do you see in it?" he wondered, and a shiver ran down my back.

"But I haven't read palms for more years than you have been alive."

"There you go again always trying to make yourself out old," he quipped, and he kept his palm stretched out.

I took his hand in mine.

"Is it bad, Carrie?"

"No, no. I've forgotten so much about reading hands," I excused myself.

"Go on," he chided me. "I can take bad news."

"You have had two deep attachments," I looked at the lines.

"Go on."

"I have never seen anything like it." I almost hurt his hand holding it, and I saw him grimace.

"Two persons you looked up to, Cy. Whom you deeply loved. One, a member I believe of your family. Your heart line. It's the most prominent of all your lines."

He pulled his hand away when I said that, but then almost immediately returned his hand to mine.

"It was my brother," he spoke in a kind of low mutter. "Yes, how apt you have described him. He ruled my life."

"And your heart," I said.

He almost pulled his hand away again.

"Sometime, well, soon, I will tell you about him. It's my only story, I'm afraid, next to the story of Gertrude. There have been only two people in my life, my brother, and then Gertrude."

His palm remained spread out before me.

"Your life line is strong, and long," I commented.

"So much more suffering then to endure," he spoke with clenched teeth, as if to himself.

At that moment, very much like a young boy, he had without permission picked my smelling salts out of my open purse and sniffed loudly.

"I've got to get one of these," he remarked, handing it

back to me. "I tell you, I can breathe better after inhaling it."

"Why don't you tell me about your brother?" I managed to get out.

A kind of shiver went through him as I said this. He shook his head, but then looking upward in the direction of nowhere in particular, he began like a man testifying in a court. "It was my brother brought me up as our parents had died when I was six or seven.

"He became both my mother and father. But he was a severe parent. It seemed I could never please him, no matter how patiently and persistently he instructed me. He taught me everything I know!

"These scars"—he pointed to his face—"are not from my war injuries as most people assume. No, they go back to one hot August day when he was teaching me to pitch horseshoes (as later he would teach me how to ride a horse and sail a boat).

"Then somehow we got into an argument over how awkward I was and I stood up to him. He was so outraged at my challenging him he picked up one of the horseshoes and struck me with it! It left me for a while badly disfigured.

"I was always to fail him, but he never gave up on me. My greatest disappointment to him came when in the war I was only a private while he was a captain in the Air Force. The last time we met was here in Chicago at the Polk Street Station. He was being sent overseas. Perhaps it was that prospect made him no longer the strict unsmiling disciplinarian. At first he was going to leave without saying more than a good-bye, but when the train was approaching he took me in his arms and told me he loved me. He was killed only a few weeks later in the South Pacific.

"That is why I often go to the old Polk Street Station. As if maybe by some miracle he might be there waiting for me!"

During the silence which followed he caught sight of a row of poplar trees moving violently in the wind.

I was so silent he became, I believe, somewhat troubled.

"Have I said too much?"

"How could you," I came to myself. "I can't tell you how very thankful I am for what you have told me."

We both rose then simultaneously as if we had heard a warning bell ringing from inside the decaying *grottoes*.

We made our way then to the path leading to the park.

"Do you think you might be ready then for going to see Gertrude's last paintings?"

"I will tell you the truth. Her paintings have always frightened me. No, not exactly frightened. They unhinged me. Maybe that's not the right word either. As a person can be unhinged after they have had an unsettling dream."

"But I will be there with you."

"Oh, I will be all right. And we do have the smelling bottle," I joked.

He grinned also then, and took my hand.

One evening soon afterwards I was looking through some of Evelyn Mae's books on ancient Greece when she tiptoed into the library.

"What is my dear Carrie looking for?"

I blushed scarlet.

"I wanted to see how the Greeks depicted Hermes."

A wave of mischievous delight went over her features.

"I don't need to ask why you want to know."

She took down several massive books written in German, and led me over to a mammoth table with a kind of lamp which in intensity resembled a spotlight.

She opened the first book to photos of Hermes whose only garment was carried over one arm.

While I stared at these photos of statues, she was busy finding other Hermes in the two other massive photo books.

I winced under her scrutiny.

As I slumped back in the chair after having painfully looked at countless photos I heard her summon Alec.

In what seemed like an instant fulfillment of her order, we were brought two tall glasses of thick golden drink with tiny little petal-like things floating on the surface.

"Carrie," she began after sipping from the glass, "we must all be with someone who, by his being endowed by Nature, takes us out of ourselves."

My lips were dry, my right hand trembled, as if a judge,

removing his heavy spectacles, had pronounced the word
Guilty!

❍

For some time I had wondered if there was some secret
understanding between Evelyn Mae and Cy Mellerick. If
true, it was an understanding, I was certain, which was in
no way at my expense or inimical to me. I knew they were
both tried and true friends.

Once I heard Evelyn Mae say we were *between Scylla
and Charybdis*. It took me some time to find the correct
spelling of these words, let alone their meaning.

There was something I did not know, and which I
vaguely saw Cy had been chosen one day to tell me. Or
was I entirely mistaken?

At any rate, I believed fully in both of these friends.

Was Cy now going to tell me something which all the
world knew except me?

Cy became queerly taciturn and serious. He would start
to say something, then quickly change his mind and say
nothing.

Finally he asked me, "Do you know Sixty-third Street?"

I made a grimace.

"It is of course a depressing street, and made more so
by the noisy overhead elevated train." But here he stopped.

"What are you trying to tell me," I said with an impa-
tience and irritability which made him give a start.

"Gertrude had many favorite places on the street where they played bebop and jazz. I think you knew she was vitally interested in this music. Wholly taken up with it."

He saw at once I did not know. Then he began his fumbling again which annoyed me as much as Daddy's pacing used to do.

"Well, supposing you take me there," I said finally.

"It would show you another side of Gertrude," he said lamely.

I gave him such a searching look he bit his lip.

"You are at last beginning to discover, Cy," I told him, "how little I know. I have never in my entire life even been down Sixty-third Street before."

There was a long quiet now between us. A needful quiet.

"In her last years," he spoke as if on a telephone miles away, "she cultivated all the famous musicians of that period."

I felt a stifling sadness in that he spoke of Gertrude's last years as if we were speaking about the world of the last century.

"We must go by all means," my voice was loud, but my enthusiasm entirely wanting.

Evelyn Mae's phrase *Scylla and Charybdis* formed on my lips.

☻

Cy Mellerick had not exaggerated in his description of Sixty-third Street. The overhead elevated train gave the aspect of permanent night. We were also the only white people.

We walked for at least ten blocks, then Cy held open the door to a saloon, lit by kerosene lamps. Its floor was thick with sawdust.

That was the beginning of my introduction to Gertrude's overwhelming passion for black music. (Later I found a book on the subject which had a lengthy paragraph about her devotion to the musicians, with a startling picture of her, surrounded by countless dark green bottles.)

What was astonishing to everybody, including Cy, was not Gertrude's worship of this music but that her mother was as unconnected with the world of Sixty-third Street and bebop music as a small child is unconversant with all the details of the fall of Pompeii and the biblical Sodom.

As we sat in these airless smoky dens with their merciless trumpets, piccolos and sweet beguiling saxophone invocations, I saw Cy's eyes watching me. I felt the day I went with him, that both Cy and I were conspirators of some dubious kind. Partly, I suppose, also because it still troubled me that he was in charge of *The Forgotten Items*. I decided he must have unknown mysterious abilities, and insight.

All at once we both stopped and looked at one another.

"Do you know who I think we are like," I heard my voice rise above the traffic noise.

I waited for his answer to my question.

"Pilgrims," I finally said.

I don't know why, but he laughed, and I joined in.

"But pilgrims of what faith?" he asked, and we laughed again.

"Wherever you take me, Cy, I go willingly. After all who knows my daughter better than you."

"Perhaps among the living," he told me. "But no one knew Gertrude very well," he added.

"The truth is, Cy, I sometimes think that I knew her less than our cleaning woman, Maud."

I saw him nod gloomily on this statement.

"You want to know, though, don't you," he spoke now almost passionately.

"I want an end to sorrow." I found this statement of mine almost a surprise to me.

He nodded again, less energetically.

"I can let you know all I know, if you will accept my knowledge. As to whether it will end sorrow, I don't know about that."

"I want to be able to accept what you know. For as Daddy said, the young men Gertrude knew are no longer young."

"Or living," he raised his voice.

It was my turn to nod gravely, even bitterly.

✿

With Cy Mellerick as my guide I often thought of Evelyn Mae as our lighthouse casting a beam out over the lake in which we seemed to be struggling like persons shipwrecked.

I wondered again and again why he had undertaken the task to guide me to Gertrude. And I wondered fully as often why I had agreed to such a task.

When we exchanged looks now we read in one another's eyes both desperation and determination. Whatever the bond was it held us.

But at every step along the way I kept muttering *Thank God for Evelyn Mae.*

Cy must have read my thoughts for he smiled and touched my hand.

If he, unlike Hermes, did not have winged sandals, he had a kind heart.

Around me I saw a terrible Chicago I had previously barely glanced at. A city of fearful energy and confusion, ceaseless change and sunless sky.

Cy saw what I was feeling, because as I learned later he was suffering the same distrust and alarm.

I knew, yes even I knew, that we were not going to these dens of black trumpeters and saxophonists merely because it was the kind of music Gertrude finally gave up her life to, no, there was another more fearful reason. Even I knew that.

Neither Cy nor I drank. We stood out in those haunts not only because of our skin color but because of our dry mouths. Yet they had learned finally, the great trumpeters and piano players, that I was Gertrude's mother, and Gertrude was for them a goddess.

Cy was waiting then for me to understand why we came to the haunts. As a swimming instructor finally sees his pupil go the full length of the pool before he is satisfied.

One night then it was me who said, "*Gertrude drank.*"

He kept chewing on a toothpick. Then his lips moved downward and his eyes seemed to shine with glycerin.

"Gertrude . . ." he started to say something and then waved a hand in defeat.

We had been to at least a dozen haunts when I saw that Hermes could then resume his journey with me downward.

○

As I would return to Evelyn Mae each evening from my hours with Cy Mellerick, I felt she greeted me as a mother might greet a soldier from some remote battlefield.

We often fell into one another's arms.

"Only you, Evelyn Mae, give me the courage," I would tell her and our silence was our bond and understanding.

After Cy's and my visit to the haunts, I could foresee sleep would be impossible.

I could see the light in Evelyn Mae's sleeping room still on.

I had a little note pad near my bed. In order to do something, anything, I wrote my sparse comments with a lead pencil.

Sixty-third Street is the principal river in Hades.

I smiled for this sentence showed the influence of the hand of Evelyn Mae.

A tar river barely able to flow at all.

The second sentence was more like myself if indeed I had ever had a self.

○

My thoughts are as helter-skelter and unorganized as Daddy's *Items*. No. More so. But then I seldom wrote them down, but remembered them.

During the weeks which followed, Cy Mellerick led me down one dreadful street after another, and from there into hidden gathering places. In order to take my mind off these excursions, Evelyn Mae gave from time to time what she called her galas.

There was music of course, all kinds, and when the young musicians tired the player pianos took over.

I sat in one of Evelyn Mae's throne-like chairs, drinking sparkling water while everyone else quaffed strong booze.

Evelyn Mae watched me with tender concern from whatever part of the room she took her place. She would blow a kiss to me from time to time and nod.

The reason I remember this one evening out of so many others is that Cy approached me with a glass of red wine.

But a young man rushing to see someone bumped into Cy, who emptied the entire glass of wine on my white gown.

I have never seen Evelyn Mae so distressed.

We went upstairs together. She helped me off with my dress, and one of her servants fetched me another dress which nearly matched.

I kept holding the stained garment in my hand, until Evelyn Mae with some of her old jauntiness said, "Let me have the spoiled garment."

As Gwen had brought back to me from my earliest days Mead Thomas, the red stains on my white dress brought back with a rush something more afflicting, something I had never dared recall.

Evelyn Mae must have heard the series of moans I uttered later that night.

She came and sat beside me. She did not have to urge me to talk. I poured out to her the story I had forgotten for so many years. The story of Gertrude's first menstruation was too powerful for Evelyn Mae to add one word of comfort or wisdom.

But her closeness made up for it.

My own words were deeper than the Red Sea, deeper than hell.

"Gertrude and I," I spoke, looking into Evelyn Mae's eyes, "were never mother and daughter again, little as we had been that before. We were never to be together ever, after what had happened." (Perhaps the Red Sea itself had parted and taken her away to another land.)

"I remember every detail of Gertrude's own private lavatory. I had stopped so abruptly at the threshold of the room. There were little pools of blood everywhere. Towel after towel stained with blood! I felt I had seen it all before. Before there was a Gertrude!

"I don't know whether it was my ignorance or terror which prevented me from understanding what I saw.

"I waited helplessly all day for Gertrude to return.

"When I went up to greet her, she did not so much draw back as become at that moment invisible. Perhaps I was from then on also invisible to her.

" 'I knew you would never tell me, Mama,' I think she said.

"I did not even have the strength to pretend I didn't understand.

" 'You would never have told me,' she went on. 'Never. When it happened'—she meant her first menstruation—'I knew I could never have gone to you. Never asked your help! Never!'

"We went into the next room and sat down. We did not speak.

" 'I went to Cousin Leotta,' I heard her voice. '*She* explained the blood.'

"From then on, as in the case of when she had burned the paper dolls, we became if possible even greater strangers. Strangers from birth.

"The time she needed me most she had refused to call on me. It was Cousin Leotta she had gone to."

I cannot for some reason remember if I told Evelyn Mae that the stain from the spilled wine had brought all this back. I did not need to. Evelyn Mae knew that the stain itself was Gertrude. And it was indelible.

○

Things were approaching a crisis in my relationship with Cy Mellerick. A kind of veil appeared to come over him. His face, of a handsomeness I had never seen before except perhaps in reproductions of great paintings, looked different each time I saw him. He was also taking from an Italian pillbox (a gift he said from his brother) tiny white pills which he held in clenched teeth before swallowing. The pills reminded me of breath freshener, Sen-Sen, mentioned in *The Forgotten Items.*

"What are those little pills you take," I spoke up after a long period of silence as we sat on the same bench in Jackson Park.

"For pain," he replied in what had an almost nasty tone of voice.

When I said nothing more he snapped.

"I thought you knew I had that. All the time." He gave a quick glance at his foot at that moment.

"You never told me, Cy, you were in pain."

"Gertrude and I had at least that much in common," he went on in a kind of soaring voice very much as if he was reading at the podium at Evelyn Mae's.

"I think I would have ached all over, anyhow though,

even if I had never been a soldier. Gertrude seemed to understand that. She told me once she was always in pain."

This statement came as swift and jarring as if he had struck me.

I felt at that moment that Gertrude herself had struck me with Cy's trembling fingers.

"Perhaps you are tired of being my guide, Cy."

A kind of thin current of air came from his mouth against my face.

"I can let you in on another secret. I think I began going through *The Forgotten Items* because I was looking for a message from your daughter. I am still looking."

At that moment I felt my search for her was at an end, that Cy was about to leave me. That I had nobody in fact to turn to. Well, there was of course Evelyn Mae. But she could only give me balm.

Cy took out the pillbox again and took another of the minuscule white pills between his teeth.

"I told Evelyn Mae, and maybe I should have told Daddy," he began, throwing himself back against the park bench, "that I would not be a good guide for you. After all, have I ever been able to guide myself anywhere but to a blank wall. My dead brother could tell you that. I often feel him around me, as a matter of fact. I am not good for anybody. Gertrude knew that. That was why she chose me. I was good for nobody but for someone as desperate as she was. We had a pact, not ever signed and sealed or even mentioned, but a pact nonetheless. I was to be with her body and soul in her words until the last curtain."

"She said that."

"What's odd about that," he almost gave a chirping sound and a thin stream of saliva came out of his mouth which he allowed to rest on his lips and chin until with an angry gesture he brushed it away with his jittery fingers.

It was just then that I realized summer had come to an end, and the fitful obstinate fall weather was taking over.

A kind of paroxysm of coughing now came over him.

I waited in a kind of paralysis of silence until the coughing ended.

"My brother always taunted me for never finishing anything I began," he confided, wiping his face and mouth with his sleeve. "So I will be your guide, Carrie, until you feel you have found the Gertrude you are searching for. Isn't that what we are supposed to be doing together?"

I was so crestfallen, hurt, yes humiliated. I hated him at that moment as I so often hated Gwen and Daddy.

I felt totally superfluous, ridiculous.

I also felt sure from the moment the wine had been spilled on my dress that Cy Mellerick knew everything about Gertrude, that is, all that anyone had ever been able to find out. He knew even what the spilled red wine on my dress recalled to me. It was a mute telltale bit of evidence like the meaningless phrases in her Record Book. That I had failed Gertrude as she entered womanhood and he held me accountable for that.

Our anger with one another I saw was necessary for us to finish our search.

Cy Mellerick had chosen to be my guide, and he was

the only one who could take me to the final place of revelation.

As Evelyn Mae might have said, then the scales fell from my eyes. Cy Mellerick was not so much any guide, he was the lover of Gertrude. I saw through it all. It was not even a fleshly love so much as a love based on the equal despair of both parties. Pain was its nature, and their love. Death, their attendant and unsleeping companion.

"How much do you want to know, just some, or all," Cy implored now.

My mind raced on, my never-ending reverie! I had to think fast, I knew if I didn't answer forthrightly I would never find out what I unwillingly was seeking. Yes, that is right, what I was unwillingly seeking. "I believe I want to hear all," I replied.

"*Believe* is not enough, Carrie. Let me say again, you must *want* to hear all or we need not be talking to one another about Gertrude in the future."

"I am ready for all you have, for I know you are the only one who has it all."

"Gertrude loved hundreds, but you know that. She had no night without love!" Cy sounded like he was on his knees.

"I don't think, though, I ever saw her when she was sober, and the reason for that is Gertrude had not been sober since she lost the only man she ever loved. Yes, I was her lover, but she did not love me. I loved her with an inexplicable, beyond the wall, kind of love. I still love her.

"But how can one love someone who is always under

the influence, not just under, but entirely drowned in it. She was drowned in booze. She had not known a sober moment since the war ended and she lost Chantrell . . . Mark Chantrell.

"When he died in the war, she told me she died.

"Yes, of course, Chantrell was rotten to the core according to other people, but to Gertrude he was priceless, nonpareil.

"She couldn't get enough to drink when he was dead. 'I wish I could drink the ocean,' she once said to me when she was near the end. 'Only the ocean's not enough.'

"Yes," Cy answered my question before I asked it, "I was her only companion at her death. I cared for her for over three months, day, night, never left her sight.

" 'Too bad I never loved you,' she would keep saying, 'because you are the lovable, the kind, the wonderful one. Too bad I could only love the other kind.'

" 'Don't tire yourself, Gertrude,' I would tell her.

" 'It won't be long, Cy. Not now, not long.'

"I brought her, if not the ocean in drink, say, a bathtub a day of spirits.

"I didn't drink, don't drink now. 'Gertrude,' I would tell her, 'you can drink for both of us.'

" 'Not even a sip,' she would joke. 'O.K., fill the cup up.'

"She died smiling at me. I had seen death when I was in service, but Gertrude's death, like her life, was all of her own splendor, for she was always to me splendid.

"A day or so before her death she made me sign some papers, I hardly looked them over. The papers bestowed on me the condemned brownstone and her condemned paintings, the paintings no gallery or museum would touch.

"So I am the inheritor of her largesse because I helped her, as she put it, into the next world.

"Yes, I loved Gertrude. I'm not sure what kind of love mine is. But it is like her death, of my own making."

There were times now when I thought both Cy and I were in a school pageant pronouncing the words given to us by the pageant organizer.

I had noticed from the first that words came slow and hard to Cy. I need hardly mention that I was not gifted in language. (One would only have to recall what Gertrude and Gwen had thought of my inadequacy in this regard.)

Our anger was rising now, as our confusion (at least mine) grew as to what we intended to accomplish.

"I want to prepare you, Carrie, for the final stage of our search," he finally said as we were both beginning to feel the damp and cold of autumn.

Even now I am not sure if it was Cy who told me that Gertrude had been a drinker since almost the day she had left home. Almost the day when she had her first hemorrhage in our home on Stony Island Avenue, the day she did not dare ask me to help her and she had gone off to Cousin Leotta.

When no one would tell her what the hemorrhaging meant, or let me change that, when there was no mother to explain it, she came to have a thirst which could not be quenched.

I realized—odd for me actually to realize anything so deep—that I resented not only Cy's being the ultimate favorite, say, lover of Gertrude, but I had always been resentful that it was Cy who was sole custodian of *The Forgotten Items.*

It was, I saw, when it was too late perhaps, that Cy Mellerick was closer both to Gertrude and Daddy than I had ever been or would ever be close to them.

I then looked upon him as one who wielded enormous power over all of us.

At the same time he appeared mild, benign, impotent, aimless, and too beautiful often as I gazed at him for a man. He often looked like a boy of twenty.

The way he sometimes looked at me took me by breathless surprise and immobilized everything I felt or thought.

○

The grave day finally arrived, the day Evelyn Mae, Daddy, and Cy Mellerick himself had more or less warned me about.

Cy and I were seated in a tiny seedy café patronized by lorry drivers.

"We will take it in by teaspoons. Or better by half teaspoons," he was saying to me.

"Where will it be today?" I spoke in a voice I myself did not recognize. Cy blinked and stared at me.

"I thought I told you," he sounded crabby like a young

boy. "Or maybe I forgot. After all, if you are flustered, what do you think I am? And I may as well tell you, if you don't already know or if you already haven't guessed. I'm not in such wonderful physical shape myself. I sometimes think I'm no better off than Daddy."

After a silence he continued, "I told you I have a very close friend. After my brother I guess he is the closest I've been lucky enough to rely on. And would you believe it, his mother is an M.D. His name is Napier."

I pretended a show of interest.

"We can always turn to her for medical advice," he quipped.

When I still made no response, he added, "Her name is Tryphena Eastlake. Doctor Eastlake."

Hearing this, I smiled a little, and said, "I had a maiden aunt whose first name was Tryphena!"

Cy Mellerick melted a little when I said this.

"As I say," Cy went on, "my friend's name is Napier, and . . . Evelyn Mae says he is really a poet, or could be if he weren't so darned tied to his mother's apron strings. He also is one of Evelyn Mae's assistants in her department of Elizabethan poets.

"To show you he is a poet, Carrie," and here Cy pulled out a crumpled piece of stained paper, and began to giggle a little as he read aloud:

Dear Cy,

So you are going to take Mrs. Kinsella to see Gertrude's heirloom house. You will go secretly, I suppose, about the hour when everybody in Chicago is dead drunk or at work in the steel mills. You will go dangerously oh so dangerously down 49th Street where razors flash and guns kill a small army to one tall dwelling that overlooks the lake. Remember to tell Mrs. Kinsella that Gertrude was in this mansion as free as larks in spring or butterflies out of the chrysalis. All she required was her easel and her bare models. Everybody else was invisible to her. Only the men standing like caryatids, naked as jays, was all she needed, all she ever saw.

"Of course"—he put the piece of paper away—"there aren't many razors flashing or guns firing anymore on Forty-ninth Street. At least not at this hour.

"By the way, he's the most notorious womanizer you will ever meet," he said. "My friend Napier!" He spoke for the first time with glee!

○

I thought of my smelling salts as I stared at the huge dilapidated four-story brownstone where, according to Cy at least, my daughter had done her best work.

We stood a long time staring at the *edifice* (it was my name now for it). I don't know when exactly I learned

Gertrude had willed him the property. Most people would have called it an eyesore, though it must have been once a kind of splendid showplace. Today it reminded me of something made by reason of its flimsiness of old movie sets and costumes. Silent movies of course!

All at once we heard music and singing. The Sister Adelaide Orphan Asylum, composed of about one hundred children who were trying to keep in step and were shouting their lungs out. Some carried banners advertising a social event to be held sometime that evening, and most of them grasped huge balloons struggling in the fresh wind.

One young boy broke ranks and rushed up to the mansion and stared bewilderedly as he kept trying to keep a hold on two enormous balloons.

Just before he turned tail and fled he shouted some unintelligible fierce words aimed in the direction of the house, but as he did so both balloons escaped from his grasp and floated upward till they reached the top of the mansion.

Shrugging his shoulders after the interruption of the Sister Adelaide orphans, Cy took out a long string of keys and walked up eight or nine big brick steps. One key after another failed to open the massive front door. Finally I heard something click and he flung open the portal.

Turning he motioned me forward.

The parade of the Sister Adelaide orphans appeared to have made him a bit cheerful, or at least resigned. Inside, whether from the front door slamming, a steady shower of bits of plaster almost like confetti began descending on us.

Ahead of us was a decrepit staircase, it must have dated back to before the Civil War. Every step we took gave out a hollow kind of groan.

Cy waited now on a step near the top of the staircase.

"Carrie, we will do this as I said by the teaspoonfuls. We mustn't tire ourselves."

"Oh well," I said, "after all now that we have Dr. Eastlake."

He clicked his tongue, and took out one of the keys from another big key ring and opened another heavy door with broken bolts.

We both coughed from the dust and a kind of stale turpentine odor.

He motioned me in. . . .

"Can you see? That chair over there should be all right."

I nodded. In the room we now entered there were about ten giant canvases spread around all the four walls. Other canvases rested on the dust-thick floor.

I pulled my glasses out of a little bag I had brought along with my smelling salts.

Cy sat down on the floor at my feet.

"You can make them out all right in this light."

"Of course, and I don't see why you were so afraid for me," I began, but then I saw the one big canvas I had not taken in at my first look.

The strange half sentences of the Record Book swam before my eyes. The Garden of Eden nakedness of the men! They appeared all at once like flesh-and-blood warm living beings advancing toward me.

I realized then that despite my having been a married woman I had never seen a man's body so lavishly, so extravagantly, so loudly, one might even say, unclothed.

I had never seen my own husband stripped down as God had formed him.

When Cy had spilled the wine on my white dress, there was an expression in his eyes which made me feel he had known all about Gertrude including the time she had fled to Cousin Leotta for help.

Today as he watched me look at the paintings of naked men, I saw the same look in his eyes.

Up until that moment I had not known Cy. He had worn many masks. Perhaps the last mask was about to fall now we had entered the mansion.

I wondered now if I would have felt any worse had I been marching to my own execution.

I kept remembering the child's balloons rising to the top of the ruined house and I felt all over me the confetti-like particles of century-old dust.

I was not prepared either for the sight of the room to which Cy now led me.

It seemed at that moment almost as large as the spacious chamber in which Evelyn Mae gave her poetry readings. The ceiling was nearly as high as that of a church. But one's eye immediately came to rest on a king-size bed, the remains of a four-poster brass affair piled high with many pillows, quilts and comforters.

I thought that Cy gave out a kind of gasp as he looked

at the bed, but then he was probably still choking from the dust.

"Here, Carrie," he spoke between spasms of coughing. "*Here* with me she spent her last days."

He went now to a closet, the door to which had broken hinges, and pulled out a handsome chair with hand-carved arms.

He insisted I sit down so that I was facing the bed.

"Who would believe what went on here," Cy spoke, as if reading now from *The Forgotten Items*. "Who will ever credit what I am going to tell you?"

I was somehow not surprised to see him sit down in front of the great chair I was seated in. Nothing, perhaps, would ever surprise me again.

My eye took in all at once a cobweb on one of the legs of the chair.

"You needn't fear spiders," he said. "I don't think anything living resides here.

"At first, after I had told her I would never leave her"—he spoke now looking into the floorboards—"I thought she thought I would die here with her. Maybe I thought so, too. But I was not ready, she finally admitted. For after all, she added, above all, it's me needs a living soul to conduct me to the other side. A steersman."

I had closed my eyes so I did not notice he had risen and gone over to a closet whose door resisted his attempt to open it.

But I had from the first noticed what power there was in his hands and especially now as he flung open the door.

I caught a glimpse of what looked like a whole cellar of empty bottles.

He brought out a tall bottle and managed to open it. But instead of drinking from it, he poured the contents over his hands and washed his hands slowly and dried them on his jacket sleeve.

"She needed every drop," he said, sitting down again on the floor. "I think the last three months of her life she could only get down champagne. Closets-full!

"Sometimes she asked me to sing for her. I have no voice, but I did so.

" 'To think there is only you,' she would repeat. 'To think it is only you can endure it as I go out.' "

I made out then a whole collection of candelabra which increased the room's resemblance to a church. Seeing my interest in them, he took out a cigarette lighter and lit one of the larger candelabra.

The smell of the burning wax caused both of our eyes to water.

"And there was no doctor?"

He shook his head. "There was as I said only me. She knew me better than I knew myself. She knew from the start I worshipped the ground she walked on, but she also knew that worship is not love. Not the kind of love she called love.

"I was better than love, she told me. Much better. And I was perfect for speeding her on her coming journey."

Cy Mellerick, I have thought often since our stay in Gertrude's mansion, must have talked all day. I even wondered at times if perhaps I was to take Gertrude's place, and he would remain steadfast with me until I joined the passed over.

"There is a feeling beyond gratitude Gertrude would sometimes say. What I have found in you, she would go on, is the only miracle of my life. To have found someone to let me slip through the veil.

"How I wish, Carrie, I could recall all she said."

All at once I saw him either kneeling or falling before the immense bed. I almost felt at that moment he was seeing Gertrude herself as she was when he was the perfect captain for her journey.

I think he was praying, no, I think he was speaking to her. No, I do not know what he was doing or saying.

Turning back he saw the state I was in, but he failed to rise.

I felt all the confetti from the destroyed ceilings was slowly covering me head to foot.

While he knelt like a communicant before some unknown altar, my eye was attracted to another portal, which looked so much a part of the ruined wall one could easily fail to notice it.

I felt that I should open it and at the same time I did not want him to see me do so. Yes, I felt he wished this door never to be opened.

He was so absorbed in his trance-like genuflections he paid no attention to my rising and going toward the door.

Unlike the other doors this decayed portal came open as easily as if a hand from within had freed it.

Entering, I found a room almost as vast as the Auditorium's hotel lobby.

But from the wall facing me was it seemed to me, high as the sky itself, a larger-than-life-size portrait of Gertrude dressed in gold sequins and shining jewels.

The mouth of the enormous portrait opened, the arms extended jangling heavy bracelets, and her soft silk skirts moved as if stirred by a current of thick air.

It was Gertrude's own voice which cried, *Mother, you came to me at last.*

❍

As Gertrude's voice died away, and as I waited in hope she would say more, I felt myself falling precipitously downward as if the entire building had not so much collapsed around me but had disappeared into a kind of mist. My descent defied any explanation or understanding in the world of the senses. I vaguely realized I had left that world. My downward fall continued. I thought somehow only of the children's balloons. The only sound was the rustle of the wings of birds. But the world had grown so dark I was sure that I had gone blind. And every sound was too loud for a normal ear to endure. More fearful darkness increased with my continued descent.

Then I heard an even more earsplitting sound like the

sea shaken by a volcano, and I knew from the excruciating pain I felt that I had plunged to the bottom of my fall. A thought came to me that perhaps I had reached the dark realm where my daughter now resided, but I knew positively she was not with me. I wondered then if I too had died, and in my death as in my life Gertrude would not be with me.

The darkness now increased to a degree that I could feel it touch me like an unearthly fog. It anointed, then smothered me.

Then just as I was sure of my own death, buried in the chaos of deep darkness, I thought I heard as if from a thousand miles away my guide, Cy Mellerick attempting to call me. I had assumed until then that he too had died.

An overwhelming pain now overtook me. I tried to touch my anguished head. A thick paste of some kind afflicted my fingers, and though I could see nothing I was certain the substance was blood but blood not the color of red, but like all else about me of a blackness which had never known the sun. The pain in my eyes became so intolerable that I lost the little consciousness I had been left with. I remember I tried repeatedly to call out to whoever might exist in such a sightless darkness. It was after one of these many attempts that I thought I heard women's voices. But they seemed to be speaking in Greek! They called in vain for when I tried to open my mouth to respond, the turbulent dark covered me again with its ever-present flow.

But after this I realized that I was now ascending upwards from the bedrock where I had fallen. I was rising through an unknown sea of fearful illumination, an illumination more painful yet than the Stygian blackness I had been afflicted with in my descent.

Again I heard all around me the sound of women's voices, but then it occurred to me these cries were those of birds for I could not believe that the realm I now was approaching was inhabited by human beings.

I began to struggle then to come awake. I struggled like the first human being who had drawn breath.

Opening my eyes was as painful as if they were being torn from their sockets! The light streaming in now was so blinding I longed again for that supreme blackness beneath the sea.

Indeed now the thought came to me I had come back from a very long sea voyage. My face and hair felt sopping wet from dribbling cold and brine. I could believe that I had been on a ship which continued to toss and turn under the sea's violent motions and the wind's pitiless breath.

Now I began to catch glimpses of faces, but faces so distant they appeared like those seen from the wrong end of a telescope, faces nevertheless kindled with animation and concern.

After what seemed hours I could perceive the blessed face of Evelyn Mae. For a moment my relief at seeing her was so great I fell back in a kind of short-lived faint.

Coming again to myself I felt her hand in mine. I attempted to raise my head but she discouraged any movement by gently smoothing my hair.

Beside Evelyn Mae I now caught sight of someone who also spoke heartening words of welcome. I was to learn later it was Dr. Tryphena Eastlake.

But it was Evelyn Mae, I do believe, who bestowed on me after my savage voyage the very breath of life. I could barely endure for her to remove her hand from mine.

Looking about me I wondered when my visit to Gertrude's last resting place had occurred. A day ago, a month, a year? Or perhaps it had all taken place at the laying of the foundations of the earth itself.

I knew I must keep my eyes on Evelyn Mae. Only she at that moment could hold me to some measure of calm. And what a wonder I knew it was that I had been restored from my wandering to her mercy and love.

But despite the warmth and illumination of her presence my feelings persisted that no blood was coursing through my veins. I felt I had turned to water or whey.

I recalled again as from an age ago that Evelyn Mae had compared me to Demeter who like me had gone into the bowels of the earth in her search for her Gertrude . . . her Persephone!

As my eyes lingered on Evelyn Mae's face wreathed in concern and generous love, I asked her how long I had been at her house. But before she could reply I experienced another strange faintness and I went back to what appeared to be a dreamless slumber.

How long I lay there who can tell.

I had sensed however an almost immediate affinity for the woman standing next to Evelyn Mae as if I knew somehow she would soon be ushering me into another sphere.

❀

"Call me Pheny!"

Coming back to myself I heard the voice of Dr. Tryphena Eastlake speaking to me. I felt her gently bathing my forehead with a pleasant-smelling damp cloth which somehow soothed my frayed nerves. "There is nothing to fear, dear Carrie." She then placed a very soft redolent lotion over my forehead.

"Your young guide, Cy Mellerick," Tryphena comforted me, "brought you here to Evelyn Mae's." Evelyn Mae, seated at my bedside, now joined in, "I told Pheny you would not forsake us! And with Pheny you could not be in better hands."

"And young Cy Mellerick?" I was finally able to articulate.

"Cy Mellerick," Tryphena replied, "is only a heartbeat away."

Some expression in my face must have disturbed Pheny for she immediately reassured me. "You need not worry about him. He is waiting for you to summon him, and while he waits he goes on rummaging through a pile of old papers."

I nodded at this mention of *The Forgotten Items*.

Tryphena now gently took my hand and began to feel my pulse. She frowned slightly and looked away.

"Let me see your tongue also, if you will, Carrie." She said something under her breath, she then lifted my upper eyelids, and turning to Evelyn Mae she said, "Would you please fetch the restorative over there on the commode."

She was holding her ear against my breast when Evelyn Mae returned with a saucer filled with a black powder (later I learned it was a homeopathic charcoal substance). She lit the restorative with a long kitchen match and then held the saucer of lighted powder under my nose.

Relaxing a bit Dr. Eastlake began to recall her own career.

"You see, Carrie, I was the first woman doctor in this benighted part of the world. But I have all but given up doctoring. My main avocation now is the study of herbs and elixirs."

I noticed that Dr. Eastlake had a soft dulcet voice in contrast to Evelyn Mae's vibrant contralto.

The lighted charcoal was then removed from under my nose, and with an affectionate pat on my cheek, Dr. Eastlake moved to a comfortable chair nearby.

I began to come out of my long slumber, whether by means of the lighted charcoal or the comforting words and presence of Tryphena herself.

Evelyn Mae, confident that I was making so satisfying a recovery, took leave of me. She threw me a kiss as she went out.

There was a silence during which I began to study my new friend Pheny. She, unlike Evelyn Mae, was still in late middle age handsome. She had a great mound of blond hair from the back of which hung down in what had once been fashionable a large switch of her own hair. She had a fresh rose complexion free of the deep wrinkles of Evelyn Mae's face, and here and there on her cheeks were a few tiny white moles which only added to her charm. Her blue eyes had such a piercing quality they almost shone a blazing white.

All at once Pheny made a remark which she could not have foreseen was to have an unhinging effect on me.

"Ah we mothers," she began. "For only mothers can know what it is to be one."

As she pronounced the word *mothers* I fought to get up as if I meant to rush out of the room.

"Carrie!" Then I heard her alarmed voice. I fell back against the pillow. A whole flood of memories—memories of course of my lost Gertrude—swept over me. I struggled this time to avoid crying out. "I was not her mother! I am nobody's mother!"

My daughter's terrible words began to strike me like hammer blows on my temple. I feared I still resided with her in her mansion of the dead. With her young men who were no longer young because like her they were dead.

Before I was aware of it I was tasting a liquid something in a solid silver spoon being balanced in my mouth by Tryphena who whispered, "This should make you feel much better." (I learned later it was tincture of opium.)

Tryphena was right. The liquid in the solid silver spoon released me almost at once from every care and pain, every tormented memory. I was light and free as thistledown.

Realizing I was now the ideal listener, Tryphena continued on, "Let me tell you, Carrie, if you will, my own experience at being a mother. For now as I approach old age I begin to see that there can be no perfect mothers in this world. Some part of what we do, for all our good intentions, will go amiss."

I was able to take in the far-off look, the strange sadness that came over her face. I felt she too had tasted the liquid in the solid silver spoon and that we were both now of one mind. I began to feel at home as if I had known Tryphena all my life.

Just then one of the servants entered and informed Tryphena that she was wanted on the hall telephone immediately.

"Dear Carrie," she apologized, "I have forgotten another patient is evidently wishing to see me. But don't think for a moment I will neglect you," she said, and she consulted her pocket watch. "Evelyn Mae will be in any moment and if you should need anything in the meantime touch the little bell there on your night table."

Tryphena then strode out.

Lying back now my eye took in some words inscribed in the center of the ceiling in gold letters:

THE STORK IN THE HEAVEN KNOWETH
HER APPOINTED TIMES.

This strange statement like the tincture and the burning charcoal plunged me into a kind of quiet reverie.

🌑

My ear then caught the sound of loud voices in argument.

I recognized Tryphena's voice and the pitched sorrowful tenor of Cy Mellerick.

"You should have known better," Tryphena was scolding, almost wailing. "It does not matter that she told you she wished to see her daughter's house and paintings. Why, do you think I could bear to look at work of that nature if say my son, Napier, had been the live model! I would have probably fainted also and I am a medical doctor. But you were right, Cy, to bring her to Evelyn Mae's. And here she should stay until she is herself again."

"But look here, Pheny," Cy's voice went up an octave and as loud as Tryphena's. "It was Carrie who opened the door to that other chamber without my being able to prevent her. For I told her from the start, she should taste only a teaspoon of her daughter's world on our first visit."

"A teaspoon of Gertrude is enough to kill! And you gave her a half gallon."

"On the contrary, Pheny, I repeat I was only following Carrie's own wishes."

"You know Carrie's disposition. She is as untried in real life as a day-old tot. Has been treated by Daddy and Gertrude as such. And yet you brought her to that mansion of death. I wonder the poor soul did not drop dead in her tracks."

I could not hear Cy's next speech, but I thought I heard him sniveling.

"There was nothing Gertrude had not experienced," Tryphena pursued the attack and she seemed to be pacing the room as vigorously as Daddy used to pace his den.

"No matter what she says in the future don't ever again take her to that ruined brownstone to disinter Gertrude. Let the poor thing remember her daughter in her own way. Now see how full my hands are! I have to restore the poor woman back to some kind of calm before Daddy comes to fetch her."

"You forget she had read Gertrude's Record Book!" I heard Cy now shout and for the first time I could hear real anger in his voice. Rage even.

"Will you lower your voice," Tryphena cautioned, "someone may be listening."

There was more talking but in so soft a volume I could make very little of what followed.

Finally again Tryphena's voice reached me.

"I want you to stay here, Cy, but keep your distance from her. I've already called Daddy and he knows everything. He will be hammering at the gates, I suppose. Let him hammer. I won't admit him yet."

Then a door slammed shut and I heard no more of their altercation.

I lay back on the pile of goosedown pillows and slowly, dreamily in fact, picked up the little box containing the tiny yellow pills. I eyed also my own smelling bottle which someone had placed on my night table.

Then almost gleefully I tossed one of the pills in my mouth and slowly swallowed it.

○

Later that evening Evelyn Mae entered my room but the medication Tryphena had administered to me made my recollection of her coming and going indistinct as an interrupted dream. And like such a dream I was not always certain I heard what she was saying to me. I do recall her gently holding my hand in hers.

After her departure I could not even recall as I lay in the elegant bed when I had had a real good night's sleep. My sleep was not to be sound even after partaking of the opium and later the yellow pills. I knew on listening to Pheny and Cy's quarrel that tonight would be endlessly wakeful. But then when had I had a real good night's sleep.

During the night I sometimes caught myself speaking in a rather loud voice the words, "Where is she?"

I picked up the bell which I saw must have been of inestimable age and fine workmanship. Somehow holding it solaced me, but I put it down for fear I should make it sound. I wanted to see nobody, hear nobody.

I was afraid to close my eyes for fear I would see myself

again with Gertrude in her mansion. And hear her words claiming me to remain with her forever.

I remembered now in more detail my struggle upward toward the light. I had denied again and again to Gertrude that I had come to her. I insisted I had only come to take final leave of her. And my coming had nothing to do with joining her in death.

At the same time I was seized with a desire to return to Gertrude's mansion for I longed to hold her to me in a kind of rapturous embrace. In the midst of these thoughts I tried to rise and as I did so I dropped the precious little bell.

Fortunately it did not ring!

I held the bell against my breast for the remainder of the night.

◠

I felt a kind of jubilation when I saw Tryphena the following afternoon. My eye caught her carefully counting out fifteen dark red drops from a bottle. I wondered whether she had obtained the medicine from an apothecary or had it from some decoction of her own. She began mixing what she called an *electuary*, a frothy liquid which when I partook of it may have been the cause of my hanging on every word she was speaking.

"I used to blame the birth of my son Napier for my giving up the practice of medicine, but I had long tired of my profession. I knew then as I know now only Mother Nature ever cures anybody. And most illness is due entirely to the sick person wanting the impossible."

She took my pulse. "Am I a little better," I asked. I tried to straighten up in bed. Tryphena kissed me on my forehead but only nodded uncertainly.

"There is no greater sorrow than offspring," she went on as I accepted the glass she called an *electuary*. "And the greatest sorrow is being the mother of a son. Sons are brought into this world to force mothers to plumb the depths of sorrow and unending grief. Be glad your only offspring was a girl.

"I know, I know"—she saw my rising anguish—"your Gertrude brought great pain, granted, but thank God she was not a son. Then, dear lady, you would have wished many an early dawn you had never been born.

"Has Cy never introduced you to my Napier," she inquired in almost a scolding manner.

"No, but ever since Cy told me about him I've been curious to meet him. Cy also read me something your son wrote."

"Ah well," she said, loosening a brooch on her blouse. "I wanted him to study medicine but having met Evelyn Mae Awbridge at the university he decided his calling was English literature and his mentor was Evelyn Mae."

After my glass of *electuary* I felt as never before.

"I don't want to tire you, dear Carrie, by going into my poor boy's many shortcomings. Shortcomings which neither I nor Evelyn Mae have been able to control. He indulges himself in every permissible and forbidden pastime. There! I've said enough for today."

I wondered later what was in the *electuary* for whatever it was it gave me a complete feeling of well-being. As a result the trials of the past night seemed to slip away.

○

Late that evening I overheard a conversation between Daddy and Evelyn Mae which pushed me into the darkest shadows of my suffering.

What Daddy was saying was high in volume: "So Dr. Eastlake believes then I have no right to visit my own wife. Is that what you're telling me."

At first I could hardly catch what Evelyn Mae was replying to his loud protest, but whatever it was Daddy's voice boomed forth, "I feel she might be better in a hospital where she can get more constant and proper care."

Then I heard the words which were to bring me to a full stop. "You mean, Vic, you want to commit her to a sanitarium." I could feel my breathing coming in short little gasps. And a slight film came over my eyes.

"Then listen to me, I will never permit you to do such a thing. Never!"

Daddy broke in, "Have you ever thought Carrie may not be as strong as you make out. I did my level best to persuade her not to search out the secrets of Gertrude's life. In vain. In vain. This all had its genesis when Carrie helped herself to Gertrude's Record Book. As a consequence she is now on the brink of a nervous collapse."

I gasped on these words.

"Well, that is how you wish to describe it," Evelyn Mae took up the dispute. "If she comes through this as I have every right to believe, she may no longer be the old Carrie who merely accepted your version of what she should believe and do. You wanted her, for instance, to accept a blank for the real character of her daughter."

"Ha, so I'm not to see my own wife," Daddy ignored Evelyn Mae's accusation.

"The doctor says she is to see no one. Carrie is in good hands." Evelyn Mae went to the defense. "Be grateful for that. She is receiving both more excellent medical care and also more loving kindness than any institution could possibly provide."

"Look here, you haven't said a damned word about how Carrie really is," Daddy started up again. "And furthermore when on earth do you think I can take her home."

"We are doing everything, Vic, to get Carrie to do just that—return home. But she is not ready yet. Yes, she is better, much better, but she is still delicate. She must be given time to come to an understanding of all she's been through."

"But when in hell am I to be allowed to see her. Certainly if as you say she is improving and you, you are permitted to see my wife, and I her husband of forty years am barred from seeing her."

"I am sure Tryphena will soon allow you to visit Carrie," Evelyn Mae spoke in a more placating manner.

"I don't know that anyone has gone through the hell I have," Daddy's own voice was now more peaceable. "May I at least stand by her bed. Don't tell me I can't."

But as I strained to hear more their two voices thinned out into inaudibleness and final silence.

I was positive Evelyn Mae would not let Daddy come in. Furthermore, I was bitterly disappointed in my husband and a realization like forked lightning came to me that Daddy had never understood or tried to understand either me or Gertrude.

○

I had never felt I was crazy, not even from the first. I knew now that Daddy suspected so and it was even clear to me that Gwen, and perhaps Evelyn Mae and Tryphena, at least feared so. But I was the only one who knew I was sane.

I had hoped in my delirium I had not blurted it out to Tryphena. I was not to tell either Tryphena or Evelyn Mae what Gertrude had whispered to me. I alone would have to discover the meaning of her words.

I was suffering fearful mental pain but I knew and believed I would come out of it if everyone was as helpful and understanding as Evelyn Mae.

I needed balm. Not hospital bars.

I had the feeling then that I was on a boat moving further and further away from shore. I was leaving Daddy for he was not on this boat that was taking me further and further into deepest water. He was on shore and I was moving away from him.

The thought came rushing into my mind that I had secrets also. I knew for certain that I must tell no one about my visit to the forbidden chamber. I had hoped in my delirium I had not blurted it out to Tryphena.

I thought if I confided in anyone I would be headed to a home for the insane. It was all I could think of the rest of the night. I was far away. Further away than I'd ever been. I didn't think I would ever walk out of these rooms once and for all as myself. I would try but I would finally not have the strength to.

No one could ever have felt more unsure of her future that late night than I. Again and again I wondered if after all I was just what Daddy had implied—crazy. And that I was to be eventually led to some secure and guarded madhouse.

As the night closed in everything was changing. I no longer feared being crazy. I surrendered to the fact that I had given up everything. So it no longer mattered if I was crazy or not. It no longer concerned me. I was letting go of everything, including my sense of time. Before this I was always counting time. Now I would count it no more.

I spent the rest of my stay at Evelyn Mae's as if in dreamland. I showed no surprise or opposition to things which before would have seemed forbidden or perilous.

I often had the presentiment that not only would Gertrude speak to me again, she would invoke her power to keep me with her in her own kingdom. I imagined then in the still watches of the night she would appear even in this sanctuary to claim me for her own. We would be sisters forever in the ruined mansion. Strangely enough I did not resist such thoughts. I was prepared for everything and nothing.

I knew time was going faster than I could keep count of. The days and nights were passing away and as I said before I had let slip my sense of time.

○

During this period Tryphena Eastlake unburdened herself of a series of personal intimate memories—a narrative of her past life.

Part of me was hearing Tryphena's words while my other part was still lost in some deep reverie. Weakly from time to time I would nod encouragingly even though my attention was a thousand miles away. I sometimes heard the sound of her words as clear as a bell while at the same time I was unable to hold on to their meaning. But my strange inattention did not hinder her storytelling. And I always could catch the sum and substance of her narratives.

She gave a graphic description of her harrowing life with her husband Dan. He lived only for one thing, the green tables, gambling. And when even they were not enough he took up another dereliction, the company of dissolute and depraved women. In order to finance this kind of life he ruined her mother's financial stability which led to her bankruptcy. He then persuaded Tryphena to dip deeply into her own resources nearly causing her to follow her mother in economic ruin. At last when Dan saw there was no more money to be extracted from her meager resources he disappeared forever.

At night there would come vivid recollections of Tryphena's narratives. They blotted out to some extent what I had seen in Gertrude's mansion.

☙

One day after telling me of the collapse of one of Napier's most recent failed love affairs with a certain Margo Byfield, Tryphena must have felt I was getting stronger because she started right in on Gertrude. "I have heard both from Evelyn Mae and Cy Mellerick of the sorrow visited upon you by Gertrude, Gertrude of Stony Island Avenue."

I was thrown off guard by this strange way of identifying my daughter by the street name.

"Gertrude after all left you to become *herself,* to become a great artist. She freed herself from you and was never a burden thereafter if indeed she was before. She did not live and breathe only when her mother's apron strings could be held to. But, Dan and Napier, they are like quicksilver running poison in my blood. I will never be free of either father or son. The gambling tables, those damnable green tables. I am afflicted as if I too sit down to gamble with them."

I don't know whether I understood at that moment what she was telling me but I still remember her words.

As she studied me now I saw she demonstrated a pleased surprise that my breathing remained normal under the provocation of her words about my daughter.

"Whatever society may think of Gertrude's activities beyond the easel and the art galleries, she was following her star! And she earned her way. She reaped stability, recognition, praise, and glory from call it her misguided celebration of the male anatomy. Her sins gave birth to triumph. Forget all the rest. Search your own narrowness. You refuse to drink from the purest spring there is simply because one tiny golden fly is seen swimming on its surface."

I made no rejoinder and it was some time before I said, "I often wonder if my search hasn't been more than my poor strength can support."

"Was anybody ever strong enough to do anything life commands them to do," she responded.

She gently took my hand and felt my pulse. "I read that the greatest American general, the hero General Grant, was so scared of battle and carnage he soiled his pants astride his horse every time he went into battle. Not that your struggle to find yourself is any less a heroic act than General Grant going into battle to save the Union. And if you pass out or even die, Carrie, you could not be in better hands than in mine."

She gave me another *electuary* to drink then. I felt my lips forming a smile totally unlike any I had ever allowed my mouth to form.

❍

It had been Evelyn Mae's custom to look in on me during the hours Tryphena was not present. Sitting opposite me she would gently whisper words of encouragement. I had lost all count of the days or weeks when Evelyn Mae made a sudden appearance carrying something behind her back which I was unable clearly to see. Then smiling broadly she brought forth a dress of dazzling elegance. It was a crocus-colored satin gown with sparkling sequins and delicate pearl buttons. She laughed when she saw the expression of delight on my face.

I do not know which of us was more surprised for at that moment for the first time since I arrived at this sanctuary I sat fully up and slowly swung my legs to the floor. She clasped her hands like a young girl.

"Oh, if you only knew how we have worried, how we have cared." She wiped her eyes and draped the dress now over me in all its sumptuous appeal.

Evelyn Mae continued, "And now I know you're wondering about Cy. He's practically taken up his residence here much to my joy and relief. He has peeked in on you several times while you slept."

"And Daddy?" I asked with hesitation.

"He's come off his high horse," Evelyn Mae assured me. "He's quit grumbling and finding fault and calls any number of times a day.

"But the great news, Carrie, is you've come through.

"You have no idea how the dress you're holding accentuates the clarity of your eyes and the freshness of your skin. You've come through, Carrie.

"Dear Carrie, I hate to leave you but you'll probably be hearing the musicians and the servants coming and going for we're preparing a grand gala. But don't overdo now. Alec will be in to look after you.

"But Carrie, oh what a change," she blew me a kiss and was gone.

☙

When Tryphena next came into my room I was seated in one of the overstuffed armchairs and sipping a cup of hot bouillon which Evelyn Mae had just sent in to me. After she complimented me on my remarkable improvement I observed a changed demeanor in Tryphena herself. For one thing she did not look directly at me and strange for her she appeared to be reticent, even taciturn. She groped for words.

"I would like to take you into my confidence, Carrie,

for when you hear what I have to say we will both understand each other better. Napier and I have had another of
our interminable arguments today. His chief recrimination of me is always my behavior years ago toward his
young wife, Yolanda."

Tryphena took my hand in hers but this time as if I
was the well one and she the afflicted.

"Whenever Napier is angry with me he always digs up
what he calls my spoiling his marriage with Yolanda
Spencer. Yolanda Spencer is as much a part of our lives
today as if she had never gone back to England. He will
never let that episode of his life die. He throws up to me
again and again his charge that I drove out the only
woman he ever loved and ruined his happiness forever."

I was further taken aback when Tryphena rose and
opened a pack of ordinary chewing gum, unwrapped a
stick and began chewing noisily. I felt I was looking at a
completely different person from the imperious command-
ing Dr. Eastlake.

"Some years ago"—she began walking around the room
now—"and I can't believe how quickly time passes, Napier
fell head over heels in love when we were in London.
With one Yolanda Spencer," her voice took on an edge.
"She was the reigning beauty of a certain advanced circle
in London's Mayfair. And can you imagine, Carrie, they
were married while I was at a medical conference for
when I returned to our hotel there stood Napier in an expensive cutaway with his bride." A flush of spite crossed

Tryphena's eyes. "There was of course nothing for me to do but accept the situation and we three returned to my home in Chicago. Napier was barely nineteen and Yolanda was fifteen."

At the mention of Yolanda's age I couldn't help recalling the lives of my sister-in-law Gwen and her friend Nettie Smith.

"Then one day after only a few weeks I found the door to Yolanda's room open and looking in saw she was packed and ready to leave. 'I've made a bad, bad mistake, Mother. I don't need to tell you why. I'm going back to Mayfair where I belong. I know you'll be glad to be rid of me.' Had I not come upon her when I did she would have left without a single good-bye."

Tryphena studied my face to see if I was at one with her. Instead, to my own surprise, I felt a sudden and swift feeling of closeness toward the young bride. Indeed, at that moment, I almost felt I was her.

I then saw an expression cross Tryphena's face as though she was not certain I was understanding her or what is worse that I was unsympathetic towards her.

"Yolanda was nothing but a gold-digger," she went on. "And like most foreigners she thought, of course, our streets were paved with gold. Once she found our Napier could not support her in the style she was used to she lit out."

But I was troubled at this condemnation of Yolanda. Even more disturbing to me I felt Yolanda must have had some right on her side. And I believed that Tryphena and

Napier were much more at fault than the very young Mayfair beauty. I wondered had I been in Yolanda's shoes would I have had the courage to stand up for myself.

I felt Tryphena was reading my thoughts. Chewing the gum she came over to me and lifted up my chin so that we gazed into one another's eyes. I saw then that Tryphena knew I was letting her down. I felt guilty that I was more sympathetic to a young runaway bride than to Dr. Eastlake, who by her tireless devotion and care had brought me to my recovery.

"You do understand how betrayed I felt, don't you," Tryphena said finally.

I saw then to both our dismay that I could find no words with which to reassure her of my loyalty.

Taking my silence for rejection she said, "Well, my dear, I'll be going. I fear I've troubled you too long with my own mere personal sorrows." She departed then without giving me a second glance.

Once I heard the door close on someone who was after all my very dear friend, I burst into a sudden fit of tears.

After a time I heard some musicians downstairs practicing fortissimo. The very volume of their playing comforted me. Why in God's name had I taken the part of this unknown chit of a girl to the sterling goodness of Tryphena Eastlake?

◉

Later I was thinking as I lay in the sumptuous four-poster bed in the guest room that I had seldom had a real good night's sleep since Gertrude's death.

Tonight I felt a certain heavy drowsiness in spite of my inexplicable betrayal of Tryphena's friendship. Then all at once I wondered if someone had entered my room. It was too dark to see clearly. Whoever it was began breathing near me.

"Silent as smoke, dear Carrie," I heard a man's voice.

He sat down heavily on my bed. One would have wondered why I did not cry out. But so many strange even incomprehensible things had occurred that this late-night visitor did not seem unusual to me.

"You've got to pardon me, Carrie, but I know we have at least one thing in common. Our *white nights.*"

"And what are they?" I asked, not positive that I was perhaps dreaming all this. I wondered too if it wasn't one of the colored musicians who had entered my room.

"White nights are sleepless nights, or as my doctor mother would call it, insomnia. I almost never sleep."

I could smell his strong liquor breath now. "You must be Napier."

"As a matter of fact I think white nights is French. Or maybe it's Dutch." As he spoke he kept removing loose tobacco particles from his teeth and tongue.

"To think Carrie, you once sang Evelyn Mae tells me in the Chicago Opera chorus. Can that be true."

"Oh well, yes, but only for a short time."

"I am here," he began now, and he helped himself to a

seat in the armchair by my bed, and flipped on a tiny
night lamp, "here not only because we are both sleepless,
but because I think you are the only person who will understand what I'm going to tell you. For I have to tell
somebody. Else I would not have broken in here like a
burglar. A love-burglar," he added, and gave a quick stifled laugh.

I could see now Napier was strikingly different in appearance from his mother, a tall man with massive hands
and a swarthy complexion, but with the same piercing almost whitish blue eyes of Tryphena.

"You and I," he went on now as I lay back on the high
pillows and closed my eyes, "you and I are not only people
of the white nights. We are mourners. You are of course
the chief mourner. Will you let me go on?"

I nodded and tried to keep my eyes open but they
seemed stuck shut. With an effort then I opened my eyes
wide and looked at him. Despite his having been drinking,
he looked cold sober.

But his left hand trembled badly, and his eyes were red
as if he had been crying.

"No one can be near Tryphena without being treated
to the story of my marriage, my first love. I don't know if
Yolanda is dead by now or not, though she probably is. But
whatever the case, I still mourn for her. And for our love."

I began to recall that somebody had told me Napier
often spoke, like Evelyn Mae, in the forgotten speech of
the Elizabethans. I turned to look at him closer now and

saw he was bringing out a half-consumed cigarette from his pants cuff.

"May I light up?" he inquired.

When I did not reply, he put the cigarette back in his pants cuff. He rose now and walked about the room rattling loose change in his pocket. "Had I only had the wit to have taken Yolanda to a home of my own, she might have stayed with me at least a few months. As Evelyn Mae's teaching assistant, however, I probably would never have been able to afford such a wife. Dimes and nickels, chicken feed, as Tryphena always describes my present salary. And as Mother always adds: If you had only followed my advice and become a doctor of medicine! But instead you fell under the spell of Evelyn Mae, where you sit at her feet day in day out instead of earning a living like a red-blooded American."

He chose another chair to sit in. "And so the more Tryphena denigrated Yolanda Spencer, the more I loved her. The more I love her still! I dream about her all the time waking or asleep, white nights or blazing days. That's why you and I have more than something in common, Carrie. We both mourn. I will mourn Yolanda forever until they lower me into the grave."

He stood up all at once, as if a classroom bell had sounded.

Sitting down again he went on, "Who else can I tell the story of my life, Carrie, but a mourner like you? My life of regrets and derelictions. You know of course, I guess, I am a gambler. Somebody must have told you, I gamble, and in their peculiar term, womanize. A womanizer and a gambler they can put on my tombstone. Can I tell it all to you, Carrie, as the night hours go by?"

He came now close to me and bent down over my face.

"You mourn for a daughter you never knew and who never knew you. I mourn for a girl whose love I could never possess.

"Yolanda told me she was leaving because I already had the great love of my life. 'I could never hope to be loved as much as you love Tryphena,' she said. 'My calling in life has never been and never will be second best. I'm giving you back to your mother just as I found you.' "

Then holding my face in his hands he came directly to the point.

"Carrie, you blame yourself for not having been mother enough to Gertrude. Let me tell you, Tryphena could blame herself for being too much of a mother to me. Let me speak out. You gave Gertrude abdication." I stared at him uncomprehending. "Don't you see what that gave her. She could be anybody or anything she wished. And she became that. She was air or winds or nothing or atoms. But I ask you which was the worse mother, Tryphena who will drink the last of the last of my blood never letting go of me or you who, using the excuse that Daddy had stolen your daughter from you, you gave her up to fame, glory, and early death. I could say Tryphena was worse because by being the all in all of my life she crushed in me any hope of being a free human being. Yolanda realized this and ditched me. Let me pour it all out to you." He pressed my arm until it pained.

I tried to sit up now but he pushed me down. "Be quiet and please listen.

"You have heard also perhaps about my latest love." I shook my head.

He helped himself to something from out of a flask. "Margo had promised only two days ago to marry me. Then of course the *letter* arrived. You need not ask from who. But you see I know my destiny. I cannot leave Tryphena and at the same time cannot stop trying to escape from her. She tolerates my truancy because she knows my attempts to escape only bind me closer to her."

As he went on to describe his latest breakup in the notorious Pump Room Bar (he was ejected by the management for his rowdy behavior) my mind went back to Yolanda.

The whole episode of the ill-fated marriage was as vivid as if I had been a witness to it!

Yolanda had come all the way over here, realized she had made a fatal mistake, that there was less than nothing for her here, and had the stamina to go back empty-handed but free. I entered at that moment into the mind of Yolanda herself.

After she had come clear across the Atlantic she wasn't afraid to throw up the whole thing and start over again. She must have known Tryphena and Napier would have kept her as a nonentity. And Yolanda would not allow the ceremony of marriage to stop her from being herself. At fifteen she had the courage to defy Tryphena and break with Napier.

I realized then that I was changing, that I was thinking

in a different way. A very different way from the old Carrie. I was like some strange winged creature coming out of its cocoon. How shall I explain or describe it, I was becoming me. I was not going to be the old Carrie of the past. I would still be a faithful wife perhaps but now I would be most faithful to myself. I was no longer Daddy's obedient spineless wife too timid to assert her own feelings and opinions.

And so, as Napier talked on, I was emerging! I believe he came to realize something unexpected was happening for he came to a halt with his story. In puzzled attention he stared at me.

After a silence, he started again.

"Do you know what Dr. Tryphena Eastlake has to say about you. She says you will outlive us all. God knows," he went on probably to himself, "I have no desire to last this worm-eaten decade through. But you can still save Cy Mellerick."

I sat up and faced him directly when he said this.

"Forget Gertrude. Do you think she needs you wherever she is now. Did she ever need you? She already had everything. Her genius and her art. But Cy Mellerick and I need everything because we've missed out on the very bread of life. We are like men who have never eaten a meal in all our years. We're famished because we've not been fed. I am past help so don't look at me. If Cy Mellerick doesn't have you he has nobody. I can't do anything for him. The drowning can't rescue the drowning."

He pulled out his flask and took a long series of deep swallows.

I lay back down like someone listening to a recording again of what she had already heard. When I looked up again I saw Napier had left me. And I recalled his phrase "silent as smoke."

Despite the avalanche of his words I soon felt lulled into an all-encompassing quiet, a quiet which ended in sleep itself.

○

I was awakened long into the next day by the sound of dance music coming directly under my room. I looked around for Napier. But then I remembered he had left hours ago. On the carpet I saw a gaily colored little package of something. It was so prettily done up I hated to break the seal. Inside I saw that it contained some gold-tipped cigarettes of foreign manufacture like those perhaps Yolanda Spencer might have smoked.

Yolanda Spencer! I heard my own voice. I took out one of the cigarettes and smelled it. Like so many other things I had never done I had never smoked. I fumbled about in the little recesses of my night table for a match. Then I saw that Napier must have dropped a tiny package of matches with the letters THE PUMP ROOM, CHICAGO, across its cover.

I put the gold-tipped cigarette carefully between my lips, and struck a match.

The kind of smoke that now came from the cigarette had an immediate effect on me. I repeated the name

Yolanda Spencer. An incredible thought came to me as if the tobacco itself had suggested it. I thought that at that moment I would have cared more for Yolanda than I ever had Gertrude. Maybe I never had loved Gertrude, and that I did not love her now.

I stared accusingly at the cigarette. I listened also carefully to the dance music rising in volume and sweetness.

Ever since my arrival at Evelyn Mae's, I had been changing. I kept staring at the gold tip of my cigarette.

All at once I felt as if a heavy iron corset which had sheathed my body for many years collapsed and fell to the floor. For the first time since I was married I was able to breathe deeply and easily.

I kept repeating the name of Yolanda. Her presence at that moment was more real and palpable than that of anybody I had ever known. If this was madness, however, I did not care if I was mad. I had been weary for many years of my slipshod sanity.

I gave out then a laugh which was as unlike any sound which had ever issued from my mouth and seemed maybe to be the laugh which had come from Yolanda Spencer as she derided her marriage and the country she had mistakenly thought she could make her own.

I smoked more of the cigarette until I noticed across one of the armchairs the crocus-colored satin dress.

I wondered what time it was and how long had I slept, after Napier had left me.

As rapidly as if I was due at some evening party I put on the satin gown, and at the same time extinguished the gold-tipped cigarette, whose trademark I observed with a smile was *Salome*.

Whether it was Tryphena, Napier or Yolanda Spencer (she still appeared to me to be present beside me in my room), I was no more the Carrie who had lived and breathed only for her unloving daughter, no, time had moved backward now for me. I was at the beginning of something, or who knows the end. Whether a new life stretched out for me or my own death was approaching I cared not a straw. I pressed the elegant softness of the gown against my face and slowly fastened one pearl button after another.

In a kind of reverie, I did not hear someone standing on the threshold of my room. Looking up, I saw Evelyn Mae. She smiled and pointed to the gown I had put on.

"I hope the noise of the orchestra hasn't kept you awake," she began. "It's the rehearsal for our Grand Gala tomorrow night. But, Carrie, let me look at you!"

She came very close to me but this time she did not kiss me. There was a kind of coldness in her demeanor which hurt me.

"Carrie, I want to apologize for not looking in on you as much as I wanted to. This fête we are preparing has taken all my time and energy. But, look at you," she repeated with even more surprise and astonishment.

"You are well No, don't deny it. Carrie, you are strong. You're yourself!

"Let me sit down," she said.

I had put out my cigarette. The taste to me was even more loathsome than I expected.

"Let me speak frankly. There are people and shores none of us can reach. Gertrude belonged to a different realm from you. You did go in search of her nonetheless. But, Carrie, she was not your daughter."

My face must have had an expression which caused her to hesitate, but then with her accustomed poise she continued, "Your mission is over, Carrie. You have completed your search. You have years ahead to be yourself and not a mother. Carrie, do *not* look back. Never for a second. Look only ahead. And you can congratulate yourself eternally from now on for what you have achieved."

She stood up, again resembling a great actress before the curtain comes down.

In the silence she began to walk toward the door.

Hardly looking around to face me she said, "I do have a last word. Cy Mellerick is waiting downstairs to see you. To accompany you to Daddy's if you are ready now to go."

She then turned to face me.

"And, Carrie, if you must be mother to someone, perhaps you can give Cy a little of your bounty. God knows if anybody can, you can give him that."

For a moment I hesitated to do what I had always wanted to do—take Evelyn Mae in my arms and tell her how much I cared for her. Then all at once I did just that. To her utter astonishment I took her in my arms and covered her with so many kisses she could hardly hear my grateful words of thanks.

"Oh, Carrie," she said in tones more like her old self, "you'll never know what happiness you've just given me."

As she left the room then it was I who was astonished. Astonished at myself.

○

Coming down the long staircase I was able to take in the sight of the musicians rehearsing for the Grand Gala, all of which brought me back to the Green Mill Dance Hall of my early youth. Pairs of dancers were holding one another in sleepy embrace. The orchestra was made up of a tenor sax, a tuba, a violin, two pianos and a drummer. When the orchestra rested, we could hear the player pianos going from another room, with lightning speed so that as the vibrant mechanical notes raced on one almost expected them to end in an explosion.

Evelyn Mae now appeared from the dance floor.

"Thank fortune," was all she said as she kissed me. She went back to her partner in the dance, but as she did so she motioned for me to go toward a young man who was staring in my direction.

He and I began dancing then as if we had been partners from time past.

As I danced with this unknown man occasionally my blasphemy against Gertrude would flash across my mind, but my betrayal of her meant less now to me than the name of the French cigarette *Salome.* And the entire forty years of my married life I saw with calm, if not indifference, as if the weight of them had slipped away forever.

Looking up now I saw Cy Mellerick approaching me.

"You won't refuse if I ask you for the next dance," he said in a manner and tone unlike all his past times with me.

Later in looking back on this evening it would seem that I had danced for hours with Cy, or perhaps with the other stray young men practicing for the Grand Gala.

"If only Yolanda were here," I said out of the blue to Cy. "Then the evening would be complete."

As if the music stopped Cy let go of me reminding me of the way Mead Thomas would quit holding me up as he taught me to swim.

Before I could ask him why he was acting so dumbfounded at my mention of the name of Yolanda, Evelyn Mae appeared to ask if I would care to have a word with her.

We went into another room which I had not known existed. I wondered even if I visited Evelyn Mae frequently there would always be a new room one had never noticed before.

"Carrie," she began, "I would not have recognized you as you came down the stairs a short while ago." She kissed me softly on my cheek. "You are completely recovered.

"I want to tell you something."

It was my turn now to take Evelyn Mae's hand in mine.

"Listen to me, dear girl, if things do not turn out the way you want them to remember my house is always open for you no matter the hour or day."

I took Evelyn Mae again in my arms and I heard a sob escape from her as she turned back to join the festivities.

Cy Mellerick had entered the room just then, and was holding a fur coat for me.

"It's snowing heavily out," he reported. "We are going to Daddy's?" he inquired after he had helped me into the coat.

I nodded, or maybe I mumbled something.

"It's going to be quite a heavy snowfall," he said as we went out the front door.

Another of Evelyn Mae's attendants was blowing a shrill whistle for a cab.

"Come in, come in for God Almighty's sake," Daddy shouted as he opened the door on Cy and me. (Actually I believe he used a much stronger swear word on greeting us.)

"And don't stand there with that uncertain look, Cy," he went on. "You should know by now you are—to quote Carrie here—more welcome than the flowers in May. So come in. And look at her Cy, if you will, our Carrie. She's twenty years younger."

Daddy helped me off wonderingly with the fur coat and shaking off some of the snowflakes hung it up on our big hall tree.

I saw to my relief that Daddy was looking well except his hands trembled still and his speech was a little slow except when he cussed.

"And how did you two escape from those two she-tigers," he inquired. "Evelyn Mae and her even more ferocious lady-in-waiting Pheny Eastlake."

I had taken my ease in one of the overstuffed chairs, and Cy put himself delicately down on a rickety uncomfortable straight-back chair.

"Evelyn Mae is giving a Grand Gala," I shouted, for my voice to reach through Daddy's deafness.

"Yes, a Grand Gala for the distilleries and the caterers! Ain't every night at dear Evelyn Mae's a Gala. And as I passed by earlier this evening the sound of the hired musicians rivaled any military band I've ever heard."

"Those must have been the two player pianos, Daddy, you heard."

"Well, if I have to go to the Gala, and hear player pianos going full strength I will come home, I suppose, stone deaf at last.

"Ah Carrie," Daddy relented a bit, "and you over there, Cy, you would leave me wouldn't you two on your wild-goose chase! I hope you're both satisfied at your exploit. I can see by your grinning you are. But on this one subject I must admit I have to agree with the infallible Evelyn Mae: You had to do what you two had to do. And so I hope you're proud of yourselves, and maybe, Carrie, you can settle down now to a reasonable if somewhat tame life here on Stony Island Avenue."

"Daddy, Cy didn't come here just as my chaperone for one evening. Do I make myself clear."

"I'm all ears," Daddy replied.

"All right then, I've invited Cy to stay with us for as long as he wishes to. But the longer, Daddy, the better. I want him to have the big front guest room upstairs. And to come and go as he pleases."

Daddy grinned awkwardly but made no protest.

"If that's the bargain, Carrie, who am I to dispute it."

"This time, Daddy, I won't hear any argument to the contrary. Cy's staying here is part and parcel you might say of my return home." Daddy looked at the carpet then lifted his eyes beseechingly to the ceiling. "You always used to say when we had our little talks, 'a lot of water has gone under the bridge.' And that saying is more true today than ever before."

"But you want to be home here," Daddy asked, "or don't you."

"I hope I want to, Daddy. That's all I can say for the present."

"And seeing the mood you're in," Daddy replied, "I would be one damn fool to argue the point with you. Let our young man cool his heels here then forever and a day. I won't argue the point. I've always known, Carrie, when I'm licked."

"Licked nothing, Daddy. You know I wouldn't stay the night if you was licked."

"So we've settled that then, I hope. And now do you see, Cy, who's the boss.

"Still, how can I forgive you, Carrie, walking out on me!"

Of course Daddy was as usual, I suppose. Only half serious. But I couldn't let it rest.

"It was your idea in the first place, Daddy, that I go to Evelyn Mae's. And I don't ask you to forgive me because

I haven't done anything wrong. I felt you were right, I had to get out of the house, get Gwen out of my hair for one thing and try to sort out my feelings about Gertrude. Sending me to Evelyn Mae's was, I came to realize later on, an act of desperate generosity on your part so I could find some *life* for myself. I had to find out about our daughter whatever the price and then maybe everything could be all right between you and me."

Jumping up just then like a small boy who hears the school bell ring, Cy asked us if we would excuse him for a short while, and without waiting for either Daddy or me to give him the nod, he took off in the direction of his new quarters upstairs.

"And what did you find when you went on your search," Daddy continued with almost solemn concern, even gravity.

"I found the real Gertrude."

"Go on," he said quietly.

"Well, Daddy, you know by now Cy Mellerick took me to that run-down deserted mansion of Gertrude's where she did all of her last paintings. Cy, who was after all as Evelyn Mae called him my guide, my Hermes."

I paused for a moment as I remembered all of a sudden what Daddy himself had said many years ago, "The truth is not for strangers." I studied him carefully.

"And then?" Daddy was almost intimidated.

"In that dilapidated once grand mansion," I picked my way through the maze of it all, "there was room after room of astonishing life-size paintings. Room after room with their high ceilings. But the last room, that one I wasn't supposed to go into for some reason."

Daddy was all at once enveloped in smoke from his pipe.

"I opened that door and went in. There was a life-size painting of Gertrude. I thought she spoke to me. I thought she said, *Mother, you came to me at last.*"

I turned to face him.

"When she said that to me and I passed out, I knew as I lay on the floor and Cy thought the worst, I knew then that I had crossed over and come home to myself.

"I knew she had understood it all from the beginning. That is, by the way things are arranged, they exist without our say-so or our own nature. We can only do for others what time and character will permit. Gertrude along the way somewhere knew that I had always tried to give her the little that I had.

"But I had never, like other people, lived. Gertrude had lived, Gwendolyn as well as her idol Nettie Smith. Certainly Evelyn Mae, even Tryphena and her son Napier. All had lived! All had at least once been alive. I on the other hand had never except in a kind of dream"—here I thought of Mead Thomas—"even once been rapturously alive. And being such a woman I had failed my only child, Gertrude. But more importantly I had failed myself.

"I knew then that I was free, free forever. I had made the search as Evelyn Mae will always tell people of a Greek goddess searching throughout angry landscapes for her disobedient and careless daughter and was rewarded unlike the goddess with only the discovery of her daughter's personality. But I learned that this was enough. I saw I knew Gertrude at last in all her shimmering grandeur and squalor, in all her triumph over her poor parents, and her effulgent incarnation as herself and only herself. For her art had given her a new birth and being which owed nothing to me or you, Daddy. She had created herself and in her death was forever free of us both.

"When I realized this I knew I could let my daughter go. Now if I do occasionally think of her it will be in the same way I think of dear friends of my early youth who have passed over. If I think of Gertrude at all it will be in the same fleeting way and without regret."

We lapsed into a stillness I had never experienced in his presence before.

Daddy broke the silence, "I feel I owe you an answer. But my answer won't be as eloquent as your description you've given in finding Gertrude. The only answer I can give is that it will take I think a lifetime for me to fathom what you've said here tonight. And though I may not understand what you've said, I believe every word of it as I believe and love you. And you were right to chide me for my comment about forgiving you. You were always right, I see that now. But then I really saw it from the beginning. And if your search is done, my search of some kind or other is also at an end."

"But Daddy," I spoke up perhaps too brightly, "let me dispute you on just one thing. You've got *The Forgotten Items* to hold on to. And you have a young man, the same young man I had, for your guide."

Daddy chuckled as he only occasionally did and said,

"By George, Carrie, are you telling me we have a happy ending on our hands?"

I held off my urge to go over to him.

"Just one last thing. Why did you never even hint that you were engaged in compiling those thousands of pages?"

"I was sure you would think it was tomfoolery."

"Tomfoolery!"

"Well, had I shown you the *Items*, those rags and patches of my young days, my boyhood, I felt it might have killed my wish to go on recollecting, collecting, uncovering and bringing to the light of day my being and my roots."

I stood up then and though he drew back a little perhaps in wonder, I gave him as surprising a kiss as I had bestowed on Evelyn Mae.

Daddy flushed and fidgeted and his change of color pleased me.

Just then Cy entered the room and Daddy gave him a very meaningful look.

Cy beamed broadly and sat down.

"Yes, Carrie, and it's our young man here we have to be concerned about. And care about. We've lost a daughter, but I think maybe we have found a son."

Daddy rose, a bit unsteadily it was true, but also without indicating he needed a helping hand.

But whether to show his appreciation of what Daddy had just said in his favor or because he feared Daddy might fall, Cy took him in his arms and they embraced as if Cy himself had returned from a long trip and Daddy was welcoming him back.

The next thing I knew they had both gone off on their way to the den where I suppose they would be engaged in a "confab" over *The Forgotten Items.*

I felt myself smiling broadly at the thought of this.

The Forgotten Items! The names, phrases and events, all of America's past, torn apart, ground up and pieced back together in some kind of order which is disorder but is still all together.

When I sat back down I noticed the weather too had changed. Had I been gone that long? For the heavy Chicago snowfall had turned to a real old-fashioned blizzard.

❍

Even the rugged winter blast did not deter anyone from attending Evelyn Mae's Grand Gala. It was if anything more pronounced in its outrageous glamour and din.

Everybody attended, not only the invited but the uninvited. It was full house to the rafters. Not only Evelyn Mae—everyone was in their glory. As Daddy had forecast we stayed not only till the dawn but the early streaks of morning allowed us to have more than a glimpse of our embattled milkman.

And so with all this behind us I thoroughly experienced the true sensation of a homecoming. Or as Evelyn Mae had put it, "The search of Demeter for her Persephone is ended."